1

The tramp steamer was not supposed to stop first at Chagres. Captain Gringo and his sidekick, Gaston, never would have boarded the fucking tub if they'd known it was headed for Chagres. They'd booked passage to Limon, Costa Rica, one of the few places they weren't likely to be arrested or shot on sight. Limon had been a good two hundred miles this side of Chagres, so the fugitive soldiers of fortune hadn't considered where the steamer was going once it dropped them off. They'd known it was a tramp steamer, but this was ridiculous. The son of a bitch captain had passed Limon in the night without bothering to explain, and then told them all at breakfast that the next port of call would be that afternoon, off Chagres.

More than one outraged passenger had suggested a mutiny, and Captain Gringo had seriously considered it. But as Gaston pointed out, Piracy on the High Seas was more likely to draw attention to them than if they just stayed aboard and crossed their fingers. It wasn't as if they were traveling under their real names.

Chagres was a shallow draft port. The tramp would heave to a mile offshore and transfer passengers and cargo by lighter, so what the hell.

Hell was a good description of Chagres. Even anchored out here on the mud flats with the trade winds sweeping the fantail, it was seven times hotter than it should have been. Gaston pointed out that this might be a break for them, as they lolled in deck chairs under an awning, sipping planter's punch and slapping the astounding salt-marsh insects that gave the Mosquito Coast its name. Gaston said, "The Colombian military are *tres* enthusiastic, for these parts, but who in his right mind would row all the way out here at this time of the year, *hein?*"

Captain Gringo stared morosely at the squalid little town across the grassy water and growled, "I still think we should have commandeered the bridge. Did you notice that Marconi rig between the masts? This damned tub has one of those new wireless outfits."

Gaston shrugged and said, *"Oui,* that was the reason I talked you out of seizing the ship this morning. Piracy is becoming most complicated since ships have begun to discuss their problems across open water. We are in less danger out here, how you say, laying low." Gaston sipped his drink before he added, with a wistful smile, "Speaking of laying, the actress I was growing so fond of went ashore with the other passengers. Didn't that attractive widow you were working on wish to keep you company in your cabin this afternoon?"

"In this heat? She went ashore with the others. We seem to be alone out here, save for a skeleton crew. Listen, why don't we just run up to the bridge, grab the wheel, and . . ."

"Merde alors, you must be drunk as well as mad!" Gaston cut in, adding, "Seizing the ship on the high seas was too risky. Trying to seize it now would be suicidal. Regard that gray vessel over there to the north."

Captain Gringo squinted thoughtfully and said, "Yeah, it's a gunboat, all right, and this tub moves slow, even when it's trying."

A tall pudgy man in a panama suit was moving along the shady side of the deck toward them, and Gaston nudged Captain Gringo. The younger American nodded without answering. He recognized the guy as one of the other passengers, an American who drank pretty well and kept to himself. They weren't the only passengers aboard, after all.

The man in the crumpled white linen stopped, stared

wistfully down at the two seated adventurers, and said, "How do I go about getting whatever it is you gents are drinking?"

Gaston reached down, picked up the cow bell from the deck near his chair, and clanged it a couple of times before he said, "This has always worked in the past, *M'sieu* . . . ?"

"Porter, W.S. Porter from Austin, Texas, if they ever catch me."

Captain Gringo stared unwinkingly at the stranger. Gaston pointed at a nearby empty chair with his chin and Porter hauled it around to face them as he sat down with a sigh. A deck steward came around the corner with a harassed expression and two drinks on a tray. Gaston pointed at the rumpled American and told the steward to go back and get three more. The steward left the drinks and wandered off, muttering to himself about drunken Americanos.

Porter inhaled half his punch before he sighed and said, "I might live after all. You're not an American, are you, M. . . . ?"

"Call me Gaston and let us have no formalities with last names, W.S. You are new indeed down here if you are given to telling strangers that you are wanted in the States."

Porter said, "Oh, I didn't murder anybody or hold up a train. I just left Austin for my health after they found a shortage in my books one day. I've been up the coast in Honduras, waitng for things to blow over. Isn't that where you gents boarded this tub?"

Captain Gringo frowned and asked, "What's it to you, friend? Are you writing a book?"

Porter laughed and replied, "As a matter of fact, I've been thinking about it. I used to do a little writing on the side while I was working in that damned old bank. I sold some pieces to the *Rolling Stone* a while back. You ever hear of the magazine?"

Both the soldiers of fortune looked blank and Porter said, "I didn't think you had. It went busted. They owed me for some editorial work I did for them, too."

Gaston nodded, knowingly, and said, "Ah, that was when you began to dabble in embezzlement?"

Porter shook his head and said, "No. I took some money from the bank where I worked because they wouldn't give me a loan when my wife got sick. I guess I should have stuck to short stories. I can *write* a great confidence game. The first time I tried it, I got caught."

Gaston chuckled and said, "One can see *M'sieu* is young and inexperienced. The first rule of the knock-around man of the world is to assure everyone it was, how you say, the bum rap?"

The steward came back with more drinks. Gaston told him to keep them coming and Captain Gringo began to worry harder. He knew Gaston had a tendency to talk too much, even sober, and a fucking Colombian gunboat was anchored within sight!

Porter drained his glass, picked up another, and said, "I know. But I can see I'm among gents in the same boat and it's good to let off steam among friends."

Captain Gringo said, "Don't bank on that, W.S. We're sort of choosy about our friends."

Porter nodded and said, "I know. You're the one they call Captain Gringo, aren't you?"

"Where'd you hear that?"

"Hell, you guys were pointed out to me when I came aboard. That's why I came back here to talk to you. I'm interested in this soldier of fortune stuff."

Gaston looked the soft American banker over thoughtfully before he said, "It is not an easy life, W.S. Are you any good with a gun?"

Porter laughed and said, "Hell, no, I only write about adventures. I met some other guys like you up in Honduras and I've been taking notes. When I go back to the states I'm going to make you famous."

Captain Gringo said, "I sure wish you wouldn't," and Gaston nodded, adding, "We are already as well known as one finds consistent with one's protracted existence."

Porter said, "Oh, I intend to change everyone's name in my book. I just need details. How did you guys get started in this business?"

Captain Gringo said, "I sent away to Montgomery Ward." But Gaston was intrigued at his chance for immortality. He said, "Dick, here, was like yourself the victim of unjust Yankee law. When I first met him he had just crossed the border a few jumps ahead of a U.S. Army hangman."

Captain Gringo growled, "Hey, knock it off." Gaston asked, "Do you want this journalist to get it secondhand, Dick? You have become a most distorted legend since first we met. I will not have it. I owe it to posterity to set the record straight."

Captain Gringo snorted in disgust and stared off across the harbor. His eyes narrowed as he saw a lighter putting out from shore. He hoped it was only bringing ship's stores or returning passengers. If Luisa was aboard he'd drag her into the cabin and the hell with the heat. He knew his own story and it was too boring to sit through again.

Gaston was droning on to the puppy-dog-eager Porter about how they'd met in a Mexican jail when he'd run for his life after busting out of that army guardhouse the night before he was to hang. Porter cut in to ask him directly if it was true he was a West Point graduate who'd served as an officer against the last Apache. Captain Gringo just shrugged and replied, "Get the tale from Gaston. He should have been a writer, too."

Gaston said, "That is true, I might have been another Dumas, had not I joined the Legion in my misspent youth. It was the ridiculous Legion that brought me to Mexico just in time to be on the losing side when Juarez took the country back from the French."

Porter said, "Hey, you've been at this trade a long time, Gaston."

Gaston nodded and said, *"Oui,* alas, almost thirty years. Our young friend, here, has only been a machine gun-for-hire a year or so, now, and already he has become more famous. Is that just, I ask you?"

Porter looked uncomfortable and said, "I don't know. How do you account for it, Gaston?"

Gaston smiled crookedly and said, "Between the two of us, he is *tres formidable.* As you know, the people down here tend to hire experts to do their serious fighting because a peon in a uniform is, after all, still a peon. I have always been considered a good leader, if perhaps a soldier of the old school. Dick, here, was a weapons officer in the U.S. Army before they decided to hang him for some obscure misunderstanding with his fellow officers. He is inclined to be *tres* noisy, but he knows all the latest ways to slaughter and . . ."

Despite himself, Captain Gringo cut in with, "Hey, just one fucking minute, you old goat! I haven't slaughtered anyone down here who didn't have a good slaughter coming! I got in that first jam by giving Mexican border jumpers a break. Since I met you I've been trying like hell to stay *out* of jams. But do you listen? No, you keep dragging me into nice safe little deals that turn out to be wars and . . . skip it. Take a look at that lighter out there."

Gaston sat up, squinted, and said, "I see him. A rather officious type in some sort of navy uniform. Probably a customs inspector?"

Captain Gringo said, "I hope you're right. What do we do if *he* wants to write a book about us, too?"

Gaston said, "A good question. I wish I knew the answer."

Porter got to his feet, still holding his glass and looking worried. He said, "I think I'll go to my cabin and do some writing. I left Honduras because I was getting cables from the states. I made the mistake of letting my wife know where I was. The goddamned bank found out about it and they've been pestering me to come back and make a clean breast of it."

Gaston nodded sympathetically and said, "Such messages do tend to make one shun the light of day."

Captain Gringo said, "Be smart, W.S."

Porter blinked down owlishly at him and the tall American nodded and said, "Go back and face the music. I *can't* go back, so I can tell you it's not much fun down here, once you pick up enough Spanish to know what they're calling you in the *cantinas*."

"I know they don't like us. But I'll go to jail if I go back. I've been thinking about giving this soldier of fortune stuff a try. It seems to be the only job an American can get down here, and I'm running out of money."

Gaston said, "You should have stolen more. Dick is right. How many months can they give you for embezzlement? Forgive me, but you do not strike me as the sort of man I would recruit for my next revolution. You have a wife in the States. Go home and write about our noisy trade. She will be less likely to become a widow if you take our advice."

Porter shot another look at the lighter coming across the water at them. Then he gulped his drink, picked up another glass, and left in a hurry. Gaston sighed and said, "Too bad. He will not live to be as old and wise as myself, but we make our own choices in some things, *non?*"

Captain Gringo asked, "Do you really think the Colombian police are after him?"

"For stealing money from a gringo bank? Don't be ridiculous. I was discussing his drinking habits. If they know any of us are out here, I will give you three guesses as to who they'd like to get their hands on. The first two do not count. Where do you suppose we should consider hiding, Dick?"

Captain Gringo shrugged and said, "It's comfortable enough, here. If they got a wireless message about us being aboard they're going to find us no matter where we are when they come over the rail."

It was a Colombian boarding party all right. Gaston stood by the rail watching morosely as a midshipman and four marines came up the ladder from the lighter. Captain Gringo stayed where he was, seated under the awning. He packed a snubnosed .38 in the holster under his linen jacket. He could die trying just as well without working up a sweat. He knew he was going to die before he let them take him alive. Meanwhile he just might get to finish his drink.

Gaston walked back to him and murmured, "They are going into the main salon to speak to the purser. He will, of course, tell them we are back here, *non?*"

Captain Gringo nodded and said, "Yeah, but they'll

13

have spotted us coming across the water. It's been nice knowing you, Gaston."

"The pleasure has been mutual. I don't suppose you've considered the option of surrendering without a fight?"

The younger and taller American shook his head and said, "Not a chance. I'd just as soon end it here, with a gun in one hand and a tall drink in the other. Have you forgotten it was just a few months ago that we almost won a revolution, here in Panama?"

Gaston grimaced and replied, "If I had, I doubt the Colombian government has. They seemed most obstinate about owning this part of the world when last we met. I wonder what ever became of those rebels we were trying to help."

Captain Gringo shrugged and said, "They got away, or they're dead. Nobody lasts more than a month in a banana republic jail unless somebody feeds them."

Gaston said, "True, and bullets cost less than food. We might buy some time by telling the authorities, here, that we were wanted in other parts. They would probably want to keep us alive long enough to collect that Mexican reward."

"You do what you want, Gaston. I don't fancy dying in front of a Mexican firing squad any more than I do dying right here and now. Why rot in some jail first? Why not get it over with?"

"Where there is life there is hope?"

Captain Gringo snorted in disgust as he reached under his jacket for his gun. But Gaston said, "Wait. Let us not be hasty. They are not pointing guns at us at the moment. Why wave our own about before we know for certain that we must?"

Captain Gringo shrugged and said, "Right. We might manage a last smoke before it gets uncivilized. They'll probably want to talk to us first. They only out-number us two and a half to one."

The American said, "I guess they'll come back here and tell us we really ought to go ashore with them. Then we'll say we don't want to, and somebody will make his

14

move. If they don't get us here in the stern it looks like a running gunfight on a hellishly hot day."

"*Quel fatigue!*" sighed Gaston. Then he stiffened and said, "Someone comes! *En garde, mon brave!*"

The deck steward came around the corner and almost dropped the tray of drinks in his hands as he found himself staring into two pistol muzzles. He licked his lips and gasped, "*Por favor,* Señores, I knew you were thirsty, but there is no need to get violent! I only have two hands and there are others one must serve."

Captain Gringo realized he was almost as surprised to be on his feet pointing a gun as the steward was. He'd acted without thinking, and Gaston, too, had snapped like a coiled spring. He smiled crookedly at Gaston as he lowered his gun muzzle and said, "I thought we weren't going to go off half cocked. For why did you draw on our *compañero simpatico,* old buddy?"

Gaston shrugged and said, "I was only following your lead." Then he pointed his gun at the glasses they'd already drained and told the steward, "Put them there and go get the bottle. This heat is most obviously getting on our nerves."

The steward put the three drinks down and said, "I may be some time, Señores. The officers are serving guests in the salon. You saw them come aboard, of course?"

The two tense soldiers of fortune exchanged glances. Then Captain Gringo said, "Yes, we did notice a lighter coming alongside. What was that all about?"

The steward shrugged and said, "They came for to arrest a bad Americano. Honduras cabled that he was aboard this ship and so the authorities here in Chagres have been waiting for him. There is said to be a reward. But will they share it with us? They will not. They never share anything."

Still holding his gun, albeit politely down at his side, Captain Gringo said, "There is no justice. You say they boarded to arrest *one* wanted man?"

"*Si,* they have him in the salon. He of course denies everything, but after they have a few more drinks they are taking him ashore."

Captain Gringo's jaw dropped. He stared at Gaston, who was grinning like an idiot. The steward said something about getting back to the salon, but his words were a blur that didn't sink in until he'd left.

Gaston sank to his deck chair, tittering like a ravaged maiden who'd just found out she wasn't pregnant after all. Captain Gringo didn't titter, but he understood the feeling. He holstered his gun, sat down himself, and inhaled some rum before he said, "Kee-rist! I'd completely forgotten that old W.S. was on the run, too!"

Gaston laughed and said, "Better him than us, *non?*"

"Well, I'd be a liar if I said *us,* but it's sort of a shame *anybody* had to be caught. He didn't seem like a bad guy, and he'd have gone back on his own if they'd only given him time to think. Now he figures to draw a stiffer sentence, and he looks a little soft to spend from now to the next northbound ship in a Panamanian jail."

Gaston said, "I still say better him than us. They'll see that he gets home alive, if only to collect the reward put out by that rather sullen bank. The rewards on us do not mention any great need to deliver us alive. I must confess, now that it's over, that I was about to soil my pants. But all is well that ends well, *non?* In a few hours we'll be out of here, and since nobody cabled ahead that we were aboard, we can assume nobody will be waiting for us with guns at the next port of call. How do you feel about Surinam, Dick?"

"Surinam? I thought we were headed for Limon."

"*Merde,* one must be flexible. I was speaking to another passenger in the salon last night. I forgot to tell you. The revolution we heard about is off, for this year, in Costa Rica."

"Fine. So what's happening in Surinam?"

"Not a thing. That's why I think we should go there. We have the money from our last job. Surinam is far from anywhere we're wanted and the women are *tres formidable.* The trade winds cool the nights and all we have to do is screw until our nerves settle down."

Captain Gringo took a quiet sip of punch and said, "My nerves are under control. I think."

Gaston nodded sagely and replied, "Of course. That's

16

why we're starting to jump at the sight of our own shadows. We need a rest, Dick. The past few months have been *tres fatigue*."

Captain Gringo didn't argue. Since he'd met up with Gaston on the wrong side of a Mexican firing squad they'd led a rather noisy life. His knowledge of the new machine gun seemed to be in demand down here, but everyone who didn't want to hire a weapons officer seemed to want to kill one. He wasn't sure where Surinam was, but if they weren't about to have a war there, why not?

The steward came back, peeping shyly around the corner first before he produced a bottle of white rum. The service would be added to their purser's bill, of course, but Captain Gringo tipped the steward with paper this time to make up for the fright they'd given him. The steward grinned and said, *"Muchas gracias,* Señor. They are taking the bad man ashore, now, if you wish for to watch."

Captain Gringo didn't, but when Gaston rose, he got up, too. They walked to the rail for a better view. The tall, rumpled W.S. Porter was standing in the bow of the lighter as it backed away from the hull. He was surrounded by shorter uniformed men pointing guns at him, but they hadn't handcuffed him. He saw the two soldiers of fortune staring down at him and gave them a sardonic salute. They waved back. Gaston said. "That is that. He seems to be taking it well."

The steward, who'd joined them at the rail, said, "Yes, Captain Gringo is said to be *muy toro*. They say he wrecked a train in Mexico and sank a gunboat in Nicaragua."

The real Captain Gringo blinked in surprise but didn't answer. Gaston grinned wickedly and asked the steward, "Is *that* who they came aboard to arrest? I have heard of this Captain Gringo. He is obviously insane."

The steward sighed and said. "Perhaps, but it is said he fights for the little people. I know he is a bad man, but I would not really mind if he gets away again. But of course he won't, this time. I must get back to my duties, Señores."

As soon as they were alone again, Gaston said, "This is rich! Can't you see what happened, Dick? Some son of

17

a species of insect *did* wire ahead that you were aboard! Fortunately, you are better known than me, so they were only looking for one tall Anglo, and since our forged passports are doubtless more expensive than his. . ."

"We've got to help him," Captain Gringo cut in, flatly.

Gaston stared out across the water at the retreating lighter and said, *"Merde alors!* The steward was right. You *are* crazy! They're taking him ashore under guard and I know the jail here. The walls are solid stone and six feet thick. But even if they were not, we owe him nothing."

"Wrong. We owe him our asses. Can't you see what happened?"

"What is there to see, Dick? They boarded with a warrant for your arrest, the purser pointed out a tall Americano traveling alone, and they made a natural mistake."

Captain Gringo shook his head and said, "Jesus, you're thick. Sure they went for him first. You're right about my I.D. being better and I've been traveling with Luisa and you. But I'm still a tall American. So how come that other guy didn't mention this when they came to get him? He *knew* who I was, Gaston!"

Gaston pursed his lips thoughtfully and said, "Maybe they just didn't give him a chance to mention it? They'd be expecting him to deny being Captain Gringo. Maybe when he told them the real Captain Gringo was back here drinking rum punch. . ."

"Oh, sure, they just took him off without even glancing our way. Damn it, Gaston, there's only one way it works. They hauled him out of his cabin, accused him of being the notorious Captain Gringo, and knowing I was back here on the fantail, Porter *kept his mouth shut!* He *let* them arrest him in my place!"

"How quixotic of him. But I can see why he did it, Dick. He knew he'd be picked up sooner or later in any case, *non?* Very well, as a gentleman of the old school he saw no reason to have two arrests where one would do. He may be deriving some wry amusement from his droll impersonation. He knows, of course, that by the time they

18

find out who he really is, the Captain and other passengers will have returned and we shall be long gone."

Captain Gringo sighed and said, "Jesus H. Christ, Gaston. Porter's only wanted on a minor felony. I'm wanted on every charge but incest!"

Gaston laughed and said, "True. But don't you see that is why he played his little joke? Porter knows that as soon as they return him to the States he will be unmasked as a simple thief. The U.S. Army can hardly hang him for killing that officer out west, *non?* Let's sit down. Our friend's generosity was a most pleasant surprise, but it's too hot to concern ourselves further with his grotesque sense of humor."

But as Gaston turned to duck back under the awning, Captain Gringo grabbed his arm and said, "We've got to go ashore and bail him out."

"Are you mad, Dick? They would hardly post bail for the notorious Captain Gringo. Porter will stay locked up in durance vile until the American consulate can arrange for his shipment back to New Orleans."

"You damned fool, they're not about to ship Porter to the States! Mexico's reward on me is more than double the one posted by Uncle Sam, and Mexico is closer. For God's sake, do I have to draw you a picture?"

Gaston grimaced and said, *"Quel tragique.* One can see how our gallant friend may have bitten off a bigger mouthful than he intended. But calm yourself. The Mexicans will know he's not the real Captain Gringo as soon as they see him, *non?"*

"Maybe. *El Presidente* Diaz and I never met in person. He still says he wants me dead, period. If you were a Mexican official with a death warrant in one hand and a fresh prisoner in the other, would you march him all the way up to Mexico City or find the nearest wall in Veracruz?"

"Oh, *merde,* Dick, Porter will tell them who he is as soon as he sees it's getting serious!"

"Sure he will. Do you remember that time we met in a Mexican *rurale* jail? They were going to shoot me *before* I became Captain Gringo, just for being in their fucking dictatorship without a passport!"

"Hmm, *los rurales* do play rough, as I recall."

Captain Gringo said, "Damned A," as he glanced up at the sun. Then he said, "We'll wait until the ship's launch comes back. Then we'll tell the others we have to go ashore for some last-minute shopping or something."

Gaston shook his head and said, "You are not thinking, my old and rare. Even if we could get Porter out, and that is *tres impossible,* how could we get him back aboard? The crew thinks he's the notorious Captain Gringo. They'd radio ahead, and we'd have to go through this whole silly business at the next port of call, *non?*"

"You're right. We're going to have to spring him from jail and get out of the country some other way."

Gaston sighed and said, "I wish you hadn't said that, Dick."

"You won't help?"

"Triple-titted toads! I told you I remembered the way the Mexican *rurales* treat people. I just said I wished you hadn't *said* it. Do you have any idea how we even start to get that silly man out of jail, Dick?" "No. We'll just have to work it out as we go."

"Jesus, I wish you hadn't said *that,* either!"

2

The evening sky was the color of spilled blood as they watched their ship vanish over the horizon. They were standing on the balcony of the top floor rooms Gaston had rented for a week. They had no intention of staying that long, of course, but the rent was cheap and people who said they were going to be in town a while tended to be investigated more casually by the local police. As a Colombian possession, not too enthusiastic about the highland government in Bogota, Panama was under martial law. With the so-called Great Powers fighting over who was going to complete the unfinished canal across the isthmus any minute, said martial law tended to be tougher than in most banana republics and it had only been a few months ago that Captain Gringo and Gaston had swapped shots with the military police, albeit on the Panama City side. They hoped nobody knew them in Chagres.

He snubbed out his smoke on the iron of the balcony and asked Gaston, "How long do you think it will take to get those papers? I want to spring Porter before midnight."

Gaston said, "I was about to leave. The artistic Italian I contacted is *tres* temperamental about being rushed. The identifications are, of course, items he keeps in stock. The checkbooks are also *tres* simple to produce. But he said he'd need some time setting up the cablegrams. Is it not amusing that warrants and diplomatic

21

papers are easier than simple telegraph blanks? One needs but some yellow paper and a typewriter, *non*?"

"Wrong. I see what his problem is. Hardly anyone has ever seen a diplomatic passport. Everyone knows what a telegram looks and feels like. The slightest difference in the size of the type or the feel of the paper would stand out like a sore thumb if you had another on your desk to compare it with. While we're waiting, we'd better think about buying some decent clothes. Let's get out of here."

Gaston shook his head and said, "*I* shall get out of here, Dick. You stay here where nobody will notice your size and blonde hair. They do not call you Captain Gringo because you tend to fade into the crowd down here."

The tall American started to protest. Then he nodded. Gaston was right. The small nondescript Frenchman was a born survivor and a human chameleon. It was no accident that only one of them had been reported aboard that vessel. Gaston had powers of invisibility denied a big blonde Anglo-Saxon south of Laredo.

He'd know what kind of disguises they'd need, too. Captain Gringo was the muscle and often the brains of the team, but Gaston was a natural sneak. Even though he was no more a Latin American than his younger comrade, Gaston could make himself *look* like one, and though his English tended to be garbled with French, his Spanish, after years down here, was perfect. He could even speak it in the various local dialects.

So Gaston left on his evening errands and Captain Gringo locked the door after him. It was still hot and sticky, but the trades through the seaward windows helped, and it would soon be cool enough to move again. Meanwhile, since he had the time, Captain Gringo stripped, tossed his sweat-soaked things on a wicker chair and took a whore bath with a string washrag and the wash basin and *olla* the landlady had provided along with a microscopic cake of soap. The clay *olla* had cooled its water to slightly less than room temperature, but since the day had been hotter than the hinges of hell, the tepid water was still warm as spit. There was a dubious towel folded on the dressing table, but he ignored it as he parted the mosquito netting on the bed and flopped down wet. He knew the trades would dry him and the sheets soon enough, and the evaporation helped. It was almost dark and he was beginning to feel human again. The town would come to life after dark, as towns did, down here. He'd learned not to dismiss the natives as the lazy folk most North Americans took them for, since he'd lived their way a while. People in the tropics worked as many hours as the folks back home. They just spaced them out different.

The Protestant Work Ethic of these late Victorian times called for a twenty-four-hour day. Anglo-Americans got up in the morning, worked all day, and went to bed at night. The Hispanics down here had long ago discovered that a schedule like that would kill any man. Green hands from cooler climes still died like flies in "The White Man's Grave." But the locals, and smart Anglos, broke the old twenty-four-hour day in two, and lived to have grandchildren. They slept four hours a night, got up before dawn to work four to six hours before it really got hot, slept another four hours during the scalding siesta between eleven and three or four, worked a bit more toward evening, then ate their main meal and got in their real screwing well after dark. He wondered if they had the usual after-dark pick-up promenade they called *El Paseo,* here in Chagres. For some reason the idea gave him a hard-on.

"Forget it," he told his erection as it started waving to him in the ruby light. That randy old tool had gotten him in a lot of trouble by rising to some odd occasions indeed in the past. But he'd just seen the last of a hot little redhead, he didn't know any women in town, and it was too hot to think of jerking off like a kid. He knew he'd need his strength for more important activities before morning, even if things went smoothly.

His throbbing cock ignored his request to simmer down for pete's sake. He propped himself up on one elbow and said, "It's no use, you silly little bastard. I'm not going to do a goddamned thing to help you."

The door opened without warning.

Captain Gringo flinched in surprise as he stared down across his erection at the woman in the doorway. She gasped, "Oh, I thought I heard you go out, Señor!"

23

Captain Gringo wanted to roll over on his embarrassing hard-on but who she was and how she'd opened the door was more important. So he asked her, "Who told you that you could bust in here, with or without my going out?"

"*Por favor,* Señor. I am Conchita Vargas and these are the rooms you rented from me. Do you not remember?"

He sat up, trying to hide his cock, as he growled, "Yeah, the light's sort of dim in here, thank God. We didn't ask for room service, Señora. Why don't you go bake some tortillas or something?"

She just stood there. What was the matter with the silly dame? He hadn't paid much attention to her when Gaston had done all the talking downstairs. She wasn't much more impressive in the dim ruby light and her voice betrayed a certain lack of wit. He wondered what a rather plain peasant with no great evidence of brains was doing as a landlady. *Smart* people tended to wind up poor down here, and she had a solid house with rooms to let.

She was still standing there, looking confused, so he sighed and said, "All right, what do you want? We paid for the rooms and I just said we don't need anything."

"May I speak frankly, Señor?"

"I wish you would."

She took a deep breath and said, "Very well, I opened the door with my passkey for to search your rooms. It is my duty."

"Your what? Who told you to search our rooms and what are you supposed to be looking for?"

She came inside, shutting the door behind her, and almost whispered, "I am a police informant. They pay me to keep an eye on strangers who stay here at my *posada*. These are troubled times. All sorts of people have come here for to stir up trouble. As to what I am to look for, I do not know. They only told me to keep my eye on everyone who stays here."

It was unbelievable. The police had hired an apparent half-wit. Or maybe, to be fair, she was a simple peasant who really had no idea what was going on. He was

24

getting used to sitting there naked, since it hadn't seemed to embarrass her. He smiled and said, "You'd better search away, then. Can you read or write, Consuela?"

"No, Señor. But for why do you ask?"

"Well, if you're going to report us to the police they might want to know if we had any passports or documents. Hand me my clothes and I'll read my passport to you, all right?"

She moved between him and the window and the red light outlined her legs under the thin cotton skirt she wore. They weren't bad. She gingerly picked up his jacket and brought it to the bed, missing the gun and shoulder rig under the shirt he'd draped over them. He parted the mosquito netting and she sat down beside him with a puzzled frown as he took out his forged British passport. He opened it, held it up to her, and said, "You see? This says I am Forsyth Hogwash Barsweeper the third and I'm a retired British major. Queen's African Rifles."

She seemed impressed as she peered at the passport. He noticed she had a nice profile if you didn't mind low foreheads. It was odd he hadn't noticed how young she was, talking to Gaston in the passageway downstairs. The deep and not-too-intelligent voice had thrown him off. He'd dismissed her as just another middle-aged *mujer* with a mustache. But she wasn't middle-aged and she didn't have a mustache, yet. Her eyebrows sort of met in the middle, but what the hell. She was pretty, in a Neanderthal way.

She said, "I will tell them you are an Englishman. I don't think I have to remember such a long name, as long as you have no guns or bombs up here. I think I am supposed to tell them about guests having secret meetings in my rooms. Don't you think that is what they meant when they said I was to keep an eye on things?"

"I can see you know your job, Conchita. Uh, did they ask you to tell them about, well, lady friends they might bring in?"

"Oh, no, Señor. Such things are a matter for the church, not the police. I will tell them you and the other señor are . . . oh, dear, what do you think I ought to tell them? I have only been a police informer a little while. Before that I worked in a cigar shop."

He smiled and said, "I'm sure you made good cigars, too. Do the police know you're illiterate?"

"*Por favor,* Señor, my mother and father were married. Not, it is true, to one another, but I was properly baptized, just the same."

"I can see you're a nice girl. I asked if the police know you can't read and write."

She frowned thoughtfully as he put his passport away. He felt a bit odd standing up in the nude, but he didn't want her to place the jacket back on the chair. She'd missed the gun once. Twice was too much to hope for. So he stepped over to drape the jacket where it would do the most good and, as he turned back, he was suddenly aware that he still had a hard-on, and that Conchita was looking at it.

He walked back and sat down beside her, trying to look nonchalant. It wasn't easy. Not having the slightest idea how one explained a raging erection to a lady, he put his arms around her, pushed her flat across the mattress, and kissed her firmly on the lips. Her nipples were hard against his chest and she kissed back with the healthy innocence of the simple little beast she was. But as he started to pull her skirt up between them she rolled her lips from his and said, "Wait! You are confusing me, Señor."

He didn't want her mad at him. Even a dumb police informer was better to have on one's side and he'd only started this because he hadn't known what else to do. So he stopped and said, "Call me Forsyth, *querida.*"

"I could never pronounce such a name. I will call you *querido,* no?"

He had the skirt up around her hips, now, and said he liked *querido* just fine as he began to finger her. Her pubic thatch was thick from her belly button down and the contrast between her and the rather ladylike redhead aboard the steamer was inspiring his erection to new heights. But as he started to mount her she protested, "You didn't explain. First we were talking about my

26

reading and writing and now I think you want for to fuck me. I wish you would make up your mind."

He got his thighs between hers, opened her body to his, and thrust home as he soothed, "I'll help you write your police report later, baby. Unless, of course, you want to stop and do it now."

Conchita sighed and responded to his questing shaft with a simple total surrender. It was great to be in her. She gave herself completely, and clamped down hard in a mindless uncomplicated orgasm just before he came in her.

Then she said, "A mosquito just bit my knee. I think we ought to get inside the nets, take off all my clothes, and do this right."

He laughed and said, "I never argue with a lady." So as Conchita undressed, kneeling in the center of the bed, he tucked the netting securely around them. It took her only the same amount of time to strip, and in the now-purple light he noticed she had hair on her chest, too. But she was curved and pneumatic indeed, and as he caressed her back he told himself there were things to be said for making love to an obvious throwback to the Ice Age. They shared another nice primitive rutting and while she seemed to enjoy it more than Queen Victoria might have approved, it didn't seem to really get to her. He felt a little insulted when, just as he was coming, Conchita stopped chewing his collar bone to ask, "Won't they think it's funny that we did this while I was inspecting your rooms, *querido?*"

"For God's sake, do you intend to tell them?"

"I think so. They told me I was to report everything that went on up here. Don't you think I should tell them we did this? I can't say nothing happened, can I?"

He laughed and said, "Well, I wouldn't want you to fib to the police. But why embarrass yourself if they don't ask?"

She moved her hips experimentally and said, "I think you are right. I am getting hot again. Do you wish for me to get on top, *querido?*"

He rolled off her and onto his back with a sigh, a little sorry he'd started, now that the first thrill was over. Making this dimwitted little thing was getting complicated.

27

There was no point in trying to get her on his side and coach her for the police. He knew she'd tell them anything they asked, including the length of his prick if they really wanted to know. So how in the hell was he going to work that to his own advantage?

Conchita crouched over him in the dark and took his shaft in hand. His thought train had cooled his desire a bit and she said, "Oh, the poor thing is tired." Then, without being asked, Conchita moved down, kneeling between his shins, and lowered her lips to kiss it and make it well. He propped himself up on his elbows and watched, bemused, as her head bobbed up and down while she gave him a french lesson that matched her other skills. She did it with no self-consciousness or protestations that she never did such things for other men. He knew that if he asked her how often and how many times she'd done this sort of thing, she'd tell him, with no more concern than if she'd been asked how often she went to confession. He didn't want to know. She undoubtedly went once a week to confession and undoubtedly drove her priest a little wild if he was young and healthy. His mixed emotions to the little primitive delayed things, but she didn't seem to mind. She moved into a more comfortable position, head low and derriere high, and was sucking a mile a minute when the door opened again and Gaston came in.

Conchita didn't stop. Captain Gringo said, "You might have knocked, goddamn it. My friend and I weren't expecting you so early."

Gaston said, "I noticed. It's all set. I got the stuff from the Italian and . . ."

"Watch it!" the American cut in, in English.

Conchita stopped what she was doing, glanced archly over her shoulder at Gaston, and said, "Oh, it's you. We've been having a lot of fun."

"I'm so glad. What the fuck is going on, Dick?"

"You can see a fuck's been going on, you clown. I've been trying to get on the good side of her. She's a snitch, but she's not as good at that as this."

Gaston said, "Ah, I perceive method in your madness. To get on her good side one gets in her inside. I am

28

with it. Let us speak Spanish lest she finds our rudeness worth reporting."

Conchita was working on his shaft again, so Captain Gringo said, to the bobbing part of her head, "We were just saying we may not get the train over to Panama City this week after all, *querida*. We have to wait for some friends and . . . Gaston, what do you think you're doing?"

Gaston had peeled off his clothes and was climbing through the netting to join them as he said, "I want to make friends, too."

"Well, for God's sake, go find your own girl!"

"Is that just? You are only using one end, Dick. The best part is back here, waiting to be serviced."

Switching back to English, Captain Gringo muttered, "I don't know. I don't want to sound selfish, but if we frighten her . . ."

Then Gaston was giving it to Conchita dog style, kneeling on the mattress. She moaned and started sucking harder as the sardonic little Frenchman said, "Ah, you see, she likes it. This is every woman's fantasy, if the truth be known."

"Oh, shut up," Captain Gringo growled. He was really disgusted, not as much with them as with himself. The whole thing was getting just plain dirty and he wanted to get up and get dressed and let them finish together. But he was almost there and he knew what Gaston was feeling and what she was doing with her tongue and . . . Kee-rist, it felt wild! He was about to come. He didn't know if she wanted him to come in her mouth or not and he wasn't about to ask and he certainly didn't want her to stop. But she suddenly did, and he moaned aloud as he felt his poor neglected shaft all alone in the cruel night air and then he realized what she had in mind and gasped, "I don't believe this!" as Conchita, having switched ends, lowered her throbbing love box onto his shaft and began to suck Gaston. The three of them came together in an orgy that threatened the bedsprings. She had Gaston on his back and as Captain Gringo's shaft subsided inside her, Conchita slid off it and back on to Gaston's. It seemed she liked variety, too.

The sated and somewhat red-faced American sat up

29

and said, "I'm going to leave you guys to finish without me." He wasn't surprised when the only answer he got was the sounds of kissing and cooing. He got up, went over to the wash basin, and started to swab Conchita off as he heard Gaston say, in a surprisingly conversational tone, "By the way, Major Hernandes says that schooner from Shanghai will arrive in Panama City about the end of the month."

The American blinked in surprise, wondering what the hell Gaston was talking about, then, catching on, he answered, "Right. I hope you told the Major the deal has to be cash in advance, this time?"

He now saw Gaston had dropped two paper-wrapped bundles near the door. He walked over, casually, moved them under the bed with a foot, and knew that if the sex-mad Frenchman didn't collapse the bed under Conchita she'd never report the bundles to the police, now, since she'd never see them. He hoped she'd remember Major Hernandes and that the Colombian Army would know what to do with the information.

It was quite dark, now. He couldn't see the couple in the bed as they pounded wetly, but, outside, the town was starting to come to life.

3

It started to rain at ten, and by eleven there was thunder and lightning. Captain Gringo couldn't have asked for better weather even if he thought God was still listening to him. The storm didn't put the town to sleep. Nothing was going to keep the people off the streets on a cool evening after they'd been cooped up most of the afternoon. But it added to the confusion and made people walk with their heads down. And if the immediate future called for a little gunplay, who was to say they'd heard gunshots or thunder?

They hired a coach to take them to the jail in their new finery. This not only kept them reasonably dry, but as Captain Gringo explained along the way, it would serve to confirm the seed of a story they'd planted with the moronic albeit friendly landlady while they'd passed her back and forth. He told Gaston, "We'll take Porter over to the railroad depot in this hack. The driver will remember letting us off there. Conchita will tell them we said something about meeting some schooner in Panamá City, on the far side of the isthmus, ergo, they'll think we took the choo-choo."

Gaston said, "Ergo, they shall telephone ahead and when we do not get off, they will suspect we told Conchita a fib."

The tall American shrugged, noticing that his new starched linen crackled, and said, "So they'll assume we

31

dropped off somewhere along the line. We did the last time we were in these parts, remember?"

Gaston grimaced and said, "only too well. I have had my fill of the Panamanian jungle, my old and rare. The soldiers who were chasing us were the nice part. Snakes and Indians can be endured. But *merde alors,* those mosquitos!"

"Hey, why worry? I just told you we weren't getting on the damned train, so we don't have to get off in the jungle."

"*Merci beaucoup.* But, by the way, where are we going, once we get this drunk of yours out of jail?"

Captain Gringo grabbed a wet window post as the carriage lurched wildly. The horse up front had tried to bolt again at that last clap of thunder. He waited until the driver got things back under control before he said, "I'm still working on that. First things first. We have to get Porter out before we can go anywhere, right?"

Gaston stared out his window at a pair of damp whores under a dripping awning and said, "The fat one's face isn't bad. I'll admit you improvised *tres* amusingly when we met before that Mexican firing squad. But, forgive me, you still make me nervous. I have never quite recovered from that time we stole that balloon to fly over a volcano."

"Look, we got down, didn't we? We seem to be stopping. Have you got your lines down pat?"

"I know how the play begins. I wish I had a better idea how it *ends!*"

The driver climbed down from his exposed seat, wearing a soaked-through poncho and sombrero, to open the door. He said, "The entrance is over there under that electrical lamp, Señores. May I have my fare, now?"

Captain Gringo said, "We told you we wanted you to wait. We have to get our prisoner to the railroad depot."

"That well may be, Señor. I am a reasonable being, but my horse is not. I must get him to the stable. He is most afraid of this storm and he keeps trying to get the bit in his teeth."

"Look, we'll only be a few minutes, *cochero.*"

"I do not doubt this, Señor. I just won't be here. They

32

have the new telephone in the jail. Perhaps they can call another coach for you."

Captain Gringo started to argue. Then he nodded and got out in the rain, handing the *cochero* some coins. He overpaid deliberately, to avoid the usual drawn-out negotiations. Then, followed by Gaston, he bolted for the doorway under the feeble electric light a few yards away. They made it to the overhang reasonably dry and he used the big brass knocker on the thick oaken door. Gaston said, "The species of motherfucker has left us stranded here in the waterfront area. How are we to get another cab down here?"

"Who cares? Once we have Porter we can walk in any direction but north."

"Oh, you mean you are not yet sure you can walk on water? I am so relieved."

The door opened. A bleary-eyed uniformed guard stared out at them. Gaston's Mexican-Spanish accent was letter perfect as he pointed at the tall American next to him and said, "Do not listen to this *Yanqui* from the U.S. Consulate. I am Don Diego Carillo Morales y Castro and my government has the greater claim as well as the greatest reward posted on the terrible Captain Gringo!"

The real Captain Gringo thickened his own American accent a bit as he said, "This Mexican is full of shit. We've been after Richard Walker since before Mexico ever heard of him!"

The guard sighed and asked, "Do you Americanos have a reward posted for him too, Señor?"

"We sure do, son. I've got my checkbook right here. So my suit is getting wet and we're wasting time."

Gaston said, "I, too, have brought my checkbook, and Mexico will pay twice as much as this *Yanqui* skinflint!"

The guard sighed again and said, "He is not here, Señores. They say they wish for to try and execute him in Bogota. They say he is a most important prisoner. So they are holding him in irons, aboard *La Tortuga*."

"*La Tortuga?*"

"*Si,* the new gunboat, down on the *embarcardero*. I don't think they will give him to either of you, Señores.

33

Colombia is very cross with him, too. The last time he was here he wrecked a train and machine-gunned some *soldados*. If you wish for to come in and get dry I have a pot of coffee brewing."

Captain Gringo was already stalking toward the waterfront. Gaston shrugged at the guard and said, "Thank you, but I must head that damned *Yanqui* off."

The guard shrugged and ducked back inside as Gaston trotted after his younger friend. He caught up with Captain Gringo under an arcade and said, "Forget it. There is no way we're going to get him off a gunboat. Look at the bright side. If Colombia won't give him to Mexico, Mexico can't shoot him."

"Of course not. Colombia will. Who the hell is going to identify him as W.S. Porter, up in Bogota? I'd sort of forgotten how seriously they might have viewed that half-ass revolution we got mixed up in that last time. I guess we made a lot of Colombian officers look silly, and now they want to take it out on a harmless banker."

"A *crooked* banker, you mean. Dick, the fool got himself into this mess. Let him get himself out."

"I don't think he can. There's the gunboat. The gang-plank's down and it's only a short dash in the open. You ready?"

"No. I want to go home and screw Conchita some more."

But when Captain Gringo broke cover and ran across the wet cobblestones for the gunboat tied to the sea wall, Gaston was right behind him. They went up the gangplank unchallenged and stopped on the wet steel deck to get their bearings. There was an open hatchway with a light inside. Gaston marched imperiously through it, shouting, "What is the meaning of this? Why was I not piped properly aboard? *El Presidente* Diaz shall hear of this insult to his diplomatic envoy!"

A petty officer opened a door down the companion-way to see what all the racket was about. He spotted two strangers in civilian dress and said, "Hey, you two don't belong here. How did you get aboard?"

Gaston struck a pose and replied, "How indeed? I am Don Diego Carillo Morales y Castro from the Mexican

34

consulate and I expect diplomatic courtesies when I board any vessel. Why was I not properly received by your commanding officer?" Then, before the startled petty officer could reply, Gaston pointed at Captain Gringo and added, "I want this man thrown off your ship at once. He is not with me. He is trying to interfere with official Mexican business!"

Captain Gringo said, "He's full of shit. I'm from the U.S. Embassy and I outrank the little turd!"

The totally confused petty officer said, "This is all over my head, Señores. Nobody told me any diplomats were coming. Please follow me to the ward room and I'll try to find an officer."

The two soldiers of fortune exchanged glances as they followed the petty officer down the companionway to a medium-sized chamber under the conning tower and aft of the forward gun turret, if Captain Gringo's mental plan of the gunboat served him. The petty officer seated them at either end of a narrow but long table and said something about a last shore leave before he left them alone for the moment.

It was too good to be true. So in case it wasn't, they went on arguing as if a member of the crew was listening. For all they knew, one was. There were pipes and speaking tubes all over the walls.

The petty officer came back with a midshipman who'd obviously been drinking. In the British or American navies a midshipman tended to be a very young junior officer learning the ropes. Down here he tended to be someone whose family had no political pull. So the middy was about thirty as well as three sheets to the wind. He sat down between them and stared owlishly as he tried to pull himself together. Gaston went into his song and dance about having a warrant from Mexico on the prisoner in their brig. The middy admitted they had W.S. Porter in the brig, but added, "You'll have to wait until a senior officer comes back from shore leave, Señores. I know nothing about such matters."

Gaston folded his arms across his chest and sat back, saying, "I shall demand full satisfaction if they keep me waiting."

35

Captain Gringo winked at the midshipman, who winked back, relieved that only one of them seemed to want to play Spanish Grandee on a modest peon lad. Captain Gringo said, "It's getting late. I don't imagine your captain will be much longer, eh?"

The midshipman exchanged glances with the petty officer standing by the door and didn't answer. Things were looking better and better by the minute. Captain Gringo said, "You boys have a nice little vessel, here. Is it American-built?"

"No, Señor. Clyde-built. We got it from the British. You must understand that the other officers are not acting as slackly as you may think. We have been at sea a long time. Almost a week, and . . ."

"Oh, say no more, midshipman. I used to be in the U.S. Navy. I know how rank has its privileges."

"El Señor is most *simpatico."*

Gaston snorted in disgust and said, "Don't let this *Yanqui* butter you up, *muchacho.* He is only being nice because he is trying to steal my prisoner. Speaking of my prisoner, where is he? One would think by now I would have seen him."

The midshipman said, "Forgive me, Señor. I mean no disrespect, but my orders were to keep the prisoners locked up in the brig until my senior officers return."

"Prisoners? You have more than one?"

"Si, Señor. The notorious Captain Gringo, some Panamanian rebels, and over a dozen navy deserters. We are taking them all south on the morning tide. That is why the others are ashore tonight. It will take us many days at sea to reach Cartegena, where the army will take them off our hands to stand trial in the capital. The captain does not like vice aboard, at sea. He said everyone was to prepare for a sober and celibate voyage by getting it out of our systems tonight. But they made me stand watch as deck officer anyway."

Captain Gringo nodded sympathetically and said, "That doesn't seem fair. Aren't you worried about the prisoners? How many men do you have aboard to guard them?"

The midshipman shrugged and said, "Enough, Señor.

They are securely chained behind steel doors and we have a couple of marines keeping an eye on the brig."

"Well, that sounds shipshape enough. I noticed smoke from your funnel as we came aboard. Your black gang didn't get shore leave either, eh?"

"Oh, the engineer is with the captain and two sisters I had better not call by name. Another petty officer is keeping an eye on the gauges, but it is most easy to keep up our steam. We have the new oil-fired boilers."

Gaston shook his head and said, "The Mexican navy would never stand for such slipshod methods. How many men do you actually have aboard this leaky tub?"

"*Por favor,* Señor. *La Tortuga* is not a leaky tub. She is a most modern and well-found gunboat!"

Captain Gringo nodded and said, "I can see that. As an old navy man, myself, I'd sure like a tour of your ship, midshipman. How about you, Señor Morales?"

Gaston said, "I am quite comfortable, thank you very much. I did not come out in this rain to inspect gunboats. I intend to sit right here until I have my prisoner."

The midshipman was too befuddled by their mock argument to remember that the tour hadn't been his idea. So when Captain Gringo rose from the table, the officer joined him and they walked aft together.

La Tortuga was a small vessel and there wasn't much to see. It was mostly armored steel built around a massive steam engine and two Armstrong turrets armed with four-inch guns. The most important features were the head of steam and the skeleton crew of eight, scattered widely at the few vital posts.

Captain Gringo waited until they got to the brig, a triangular area above the chain lockers and under the steel deck of the prow, before he made his move. The midshipman had just led him into the little guard room and introduced him to the two marines seated under a light in front of the two solid cell doors when the tall American pulled his .38 and said, "All right, *muchachos.* Everybody keep their hands polite. Who's got the keys to those cells?"

One of the marines swore and grabbed for his holstered six-gun as he rose. Captain Gringo fired. The

37

slug hit the man between his front teeth and spattered bone, blood, and brain onto the gray steel behind him. As the body thudded to the deck the other marine put both palms against the low overhead and gasped, "I have the keys, Señor! For the love of God, my mother needs me!"

The midshipman was frozen in place as silent as a rooted tree. The American said, "As I was saying, first we open the doors, right?"

The marine, still breathing, said, "*Si,* Señor. But I have for to lower my hands to do it, no?"

"Just avoid sudden moves and we'll get along. Which door are you holding the American prisoner behind?"

"This one, Señor. They put him in with the rebels. The deserters are next door."

"Right. Let the American out and put the keys on the floor. I want you both over in that far corner for the moment. You can move now, midshipman."

The middy frowned as if he was having a bad dream and was wondering why he couldn't wake up. He said, "This is piracy, Señor. I won't have it!"

"Would you rather have a bullet in the guts?"

"Well, since you put it that way." He sighed, and stepped over to stand in the corner like a chastised child.

The marine unlocked the cell door, dropped the key ring, and stepped over to stand by the midshipman. Captain Gringo yelled, "Are you in there, Porter?" in English, and the door opened a crack. W.S. Porter stuck a pale face out, gasped at the sight of the body, and said, "Jesus H. Christ! It's you! What's the story, Walker?"

"Some day you can write it. Pick up that pistol from the stiff and cover those guys over there."

"Walker, I'm not very good at this."

"Shut up and do as you're told. We risked our tails to get you out of that cell. If you fuck up we'll put you back where we found you."

Porter grimaced, knelt by the messy corpse, and rose with a gun in his soft hand. He grinned sheepishly and said, "All right, you guys. I had a drink with Buffalo Bill one time, so don't you mess with me."

As Porter covered the crew members, Captain Gringo

called out in Spanish, "Rebels out, single file and lined up for inspection against the bulkhead."

Nothing happened. Porter said, "They're chained up in there, Dick."

"Shit. How come *you* weren't?"

"I was. This guy I used to know in Texas showed me how to pick locks with a hairpin, so. . ."

Captain Gringo didn't care where Porter had found a hairpin, so he stepped over to the cell door, kneeling along the way to pick up the keys. He stepped inside, squinting in the dim light, and a man seated against the wall sighed, "Viva Captain Gringo!"

There were twelve of them, ten men and two women. He felt better about shooting that marine when he saw all of them were chained to the walls. An empty set of irons hung near one of the women, so he knew where Porter had gotten the hairpin, and that the girl could stay cool while another prisoner was trying to escape. He handed her the keys and said, "Free yourself and unlock the others, Señorita. You all heard what I said. So let's move it."

As he started to rejoin Porter one of the dimly visible men asked, "Don't you remember me, Captain? I am Jesus Gomez, from the old brigade!"

The American started to answer. Then he stiffened as the sound of gunshots filled the air and tingled the steel all around. He ducked out the doorway, his own gun ready for anything, to see Porter standing there with a smoking pistol, staring down in utter horror at the two bodies at his feet. Porter gasped, "They tried to jump me. It all happened so fast."

"My fault. I should have known they'd take advantage of your limited Spanish."

"Jesus, they did mutter back and forth too fast for me to savvy. Do you think they're dead?"

"I hope so. It saves a lot of complications if you did it right."

They both turned as Gaston came in, wiping his switch blade with a seaman's hat. Gaston glanced down and said, "I *thought* those shots came from this direction. Fortunately, it is hard to tell in a thunderstorm. Don't you think we'd better consider going ashore now Dick?"

The rebel prisoners were filing out, rubbing their chaffed wrists and blinking at the light and bodies. Captain Gringo said, "I see you didn't bring that petty officer with you. What happened?"

Gaston shrugged and said, "He said something stupid about getting someone when we heard the first shot. It does not sound like thunder when you fire almost next door. Fortunately, he did not consider that we might be on the same side, so he made the tactical error of turning his back on me when he decided to call for help. You really should allow me to teach you the finer points of knife fighting, Dick. Your methods are effective, but so noisy."

"I've noticed that. What about the rest of the crew?"

"I took the liberty of locking a few bulkheads from this side. There was only one man posted between here and the gangplank. This is his hat. I see we have rescued our friend and some others for reasons you can explain as we go our merry way. What are we waiting for, Dick?"

"I'm thinking."

Mon Dieu, I wish you wouldn't. The damned crew may be arriving at any minute and one's improvised explanations can only carry one so far."

Porter was getting over his shock and said, "He's right. Let's get the hell out of here."

But Captain Gringo stared at the prisoners he'd released and asked, "Have any of you guys ever served aboard a ship before?"

Two of them raised their hands. Gaston asked, "What do you mean, *before,* Dick? If you are thinking what I think you're thinking, forget it! I won't go to sea in a stolen gunboat, with or without a crew!"

Captain Gringo nodded. Then he stepped over to the other cell door and unlocked it. As he expected, the sailors inside were chained to the bulkheads. They were staring up at him with mingled hope and apathy as he said, "I am called Captain Gringo and I just seized this vessel. If any of you want to be put ashore it's all right wih us. You might duck the shore patrols. You may not. If any of you want to help us take this tub out of here,

40

speak up. I need a couple of good helmsmen and somebody who knows a steam engine from a sewing machine."

Jesus Gomez joined him in the doorway to shout, *"Viva la revolucion!* I know this man, *muchachos!* He always wins!"

One of the chained seamen said, "I know a steam engine from a sewing machine. I used to be a chief petty officer, before a damned ensign got fresh with my woman."

Others started to enumerate their skills as Captain Gringo handed the keys to Gomez and told him to get them on their feet. He ducked back outside and told Gaston, "Okay, we have a crew, sort of. I know where the arms locker is and the midshipman had a key. Let's spread some guns around and move it out."

Gaston said, "Dick, this is piracy."

"So what? How many times can they hang us?"

"I'm not talking about these banana republics, damn it. If we take this boat we'll have the whole world after us. The French, the Dutch, the British, and the U.S. Navy are patrolling the Caribbean just over the horizon. They'll hear what we've done by wireless and close in on all sides for the kill!"

Captain Gringo shrugged and said, "I know. But it sure beats walking, and, what the hell, it's a gunboat, isn't it?"

4

Despite some confusion on the part of his mixed crew, and with the help of the thunderstorm, it only took another twenty minutes or so before they were ready to cast off. Gaston had objected to turning the survivors of the original crew loose, but the choice was between shooting them or casting them adrift later in a lifeboat off the mangrove- and cannibal-infested Mosquito Coast. Captain Gringo made it a policy never to kill anyone he didn't have to, and the thoroughly cowed survivors gave him no lip at all as he ran them down the gangplank. The machine gun he'd taken from the arms locker and positioned near the gangplank seemed to speed their departure. Captain Gringo chuckled fondly as the last of them vanished in the rain, and he called out, "All right, prepare to cast off. Gaston, run up and make sure that helmsman knows what he's doing. Head straight out to sea and I'll join you after a quick check."

Gaston muttered, *"Merde,"* and left him there with Porter and a couple of the released rebel prisoners. Captain Gringo turned to them and said, "If you guys don't want to go ashore, let's think about hauling in that gangplank, shall we?"

One of them licked his lips and said, "I have never been to sea, Señor. Is it true there are sharks out there?" "Sharks and probably some battleships who bite even harder. All ashore who's going ashore."

The man shuddered and said, "If we go with you

we will probably drown and be eaten by sharks. If we go ashore we will certainly be shot. I hope I do not get seasick."

Captain Gringo said, "You probably will. Let's haul away."

Porter suddenly gasped and said, "Oh, oh! Company!"

Captain Gringo turned to peer at the skirmish line of dark figures moving their way across the cobblestones of the wide *embarcadero*. A blossom of flame indicated at least one of them was trigger happy, but the bullet whined too close overhead for comfort. Captain Gringo said, "Everybody down. Take cover. Porter," as he dropped behind the machine gun. Porter hunkered at his side, behind the meager shelter of the unarmored rail, and asked, "What about the gangplank?"

Captain Gringo said, "Screw the gangplank," and opened up with the machine gun as others in the attacking party opened up with their side arms.

The machine gun was a Belgian-made Maxim .30– 30, and up in the conning tower, Gaston took the hint as he heard its savage woodpecker rattle. The deck began to shudder under them as the twin screws churned white water. The man they'd sent aft to cast off the stern line had ducked for cover without doing his job when he saw the shore patrol coming. But the lines began to pop with twangs even louder than the gunshots from both sides, and *La Tortuga* was moving. She moved with maddening slowness at first, as the engine fought the inertia of her heavy mass. Someone ashore with more courage than brains saw what was happening and led, or ordered, an all-out charge!

Captain Gringo hosed them with hot lead as they came and men went down to wriggle like earthworms on a hot stove as Porter buried his face in his hands and sobbed, "Jesus, stop it. You're killing them!"

Captain Gringo ceased fire, ears ringing, and said, "That's the general idea. But we're out of range, now. I think we made it, W.S. By the way, what do the initials stand for?"

"Call me Bill. I don't feel much like a banker these

43

days. You're incredible. You must have just put a dozen of them on the ground and you're still cool as a cucumber. Doesn't it get to you, Dick?"

Captain Gringo began to replace the Maxim's belt as he said, "It used to. How do you feel about those guys you shot, up forward?"

"That's different. I had no choice when they jumped me."

"What do you think those fuckers back there were trying to do, take our temperatures? This soldier-of-fortune shit sounds like a lot of fun. A lot of us wanted to grow up to be pirates, too. But the game is played for keeps in the real world. Those guys back there weren't out to win our marbles. If it's any comfort to you, they knew I didn't want *their* marbles either."

Porter licked his lips and said, "So it's kill or be killed. It sounds spookier when you say it for *real!* Where are we going, now?"

Captain Gringo said, "First things first. I'm going to inspect the watch and make sure we're going *anywhere.* Then we'll join Gaston at the helm and figure out a course. I want everyone ashore to remember us headed straight out to sea. So we don't have to worry about turning until we're well over the horizon in the dark."

"That makes sense, I think. Just so we don't head for Honduras. They're looking for me there."

Captain Gringo said, "I know. They're after me everywhere. I guess our best bet is the Gulf of Darien."

"I never heard of it. Do you suppose they have an extradition treaty with the States? Who lives there?"

"Nobody. That's why it's our best bet. The Gulf of Darien is a blind alley between the South American mainland and the bad end of Central America. The early explorers thought you could work a ship through those swamps to the Pacific side. The early explorers died a lot. I understand it's a real hell hole. The Spaniards gave up soon after they took a good look at it. I read that some Scottish settlers tried to found a colony there, couple of hundred years ago. It didn't work out so good. Jungle fevers killed off the few Scots the Indians failed to."

44

Porter grimaced and said, "Glugh! You paint a lovely picture. Why in the hell do you want to head for such a place, Dick?"

"Shit, they'll be looking for us in all the *pretty* places. Nobody lives along the Gulf of Darien but crocodiles and man-eating jungle natives. The offshore shoals are treacherous and the bugs are supposed to grow so big they eat birds on the wing. Would *you* send a shore patrol into a place like that?"

"I don't imagine I would. But what if the natives and other monsters decide they want to eat us, Dick?"

"Shit, the poor Highlanders of the old Darien Expedition had to fight things off with flintlocks and claymores. We're packing four-inch guns fore and aft."

He rose, with the machine gun cradled in his arms, and added, "Let's go." Porter asked why he was taking the machine gun to the bridge, and he sighed, "I'm putting it back in the arms locker, damn it. You can't leave a freshly fired gun out on deck in this sea air. Do you know how to clean a gun, Bill?"

"Well, I've cleaned a few shotguns and rifles in my time. I've never seen the insides of a machine gun."

"Few people have. They're still a novelty. I'd better show you how to field-strip and clean a Maxim. You're going to have to do something to earn your keep, and we don't have any bank aboard this tub."

"If there was, you'd have robbed it, right?"

"Wrong. I'm a professional soldier. *You're* the guy that robs banks." They were entering the superstructure, now, and Porter's face was flushed as he said, "See here, Walker!" But Captain Gringo cut him off with, "No. *You* see here, you pious bastard! We owed you, so we saved you from a certain execution you wouldn't have been able to laugh off. I'd do it again if I had to, especially now that I see they had a dozen other *pobrecitos* lined up for a Bogota necktie party. But let's get a few things straight. I'm, well, a killer, if you want to put it that way. You're a con man and a thief. So be it. I know guys like you justify their game by pointing to guys like Gaston and me as the real villains. You gentle grafters really never hurt anybody, right? Oh, sure, you may sell

45

a gold brick here and slip a few bucks out of a pocket there, but you're above violence. You've never shot or stabbed anybody."

Porter looked down and murmured, "Not until a few minutes ago."

Captain Gringo led the way into the arms locker and placed the Maxim on a workbench. Then he turned and said, "Okay, Gaston and me are paid killers. We shoot and stab and blow people to hash for a living. But every son of a bitch we've killed was another pro, like us, or a bandit or unreconstructed Indian."

"I assume there's a point to this lecture?"

"You're damned A. I'm talking about hurting people for money. I guess Gaston and me have made a few widows and orphans, but we've never *robbed* any! You were entrusted with the money of innocent people who'd never lifted a finger against you. You stole it. You didn't point a gun. You didn't even raise your voice. You just grinned like a shiteating dog and walked off with their savings. So how do you think they must feel about you right now?"

Porter blanched, balled his fists, and looked like he was about to start swinging. Captain Gringo said, "Don't," and the pudgy banker lowered his head and sniffed, "I really needed it, Dick. My wife, Athol, was really sick."

Captain Gringo nodded and said, "I'll buy that, Bill. I've had to do some shitty things and I don't even have a wife. My point is that we all do shitty things, sometimes, and to stay alive can really get shitty."

Porter sniffed again and asked, "Then why in the hell are you all riled up at me?"

"I'm not sure. I think you were calling the shots too close for my comfort, too. That way you have of laughing off your own sins while sneering at everyone else's is annoying as hell, Bill."

Porter raised his face and his eyes were filled with agony as he blurted, "Can't you see I laugh to keep from crying? For God's sake, don't you think I *know* what the people who trusted me think of me right now? You're a strong man, Dick. You can face up to life the way it is. I can't. I'm weak. I've hidden that behind a false front

46

and a joshing way of talking until sometimes I forget how small I feel. I blew a good job and left a dying wife to run off, scared and drunk. I drink too much and I lie when the truth is in my favor. You're not the first cuss who's called me on the way I have of making others feel small with my mouth. I damned near got killed in West Texas as a kid, trying to be a tough trail hand and bragging myself into fights I wound up running from. I don't know *why* I tell some of the fool stories I make up about myself."

Captain Gringo opened the breechblock as he nodded and said, "You ought to write them down. I've been meaning to ask you. Why in hell did you let them arrest you in my place? We'd only met, and you must have known as soon as they started talking that they didn't have a warrant out on you."

Porter sat on a box, ran his fingers through his hair, and said, "I've been wondering ever since I did it. I must be crazy. They took me from my cabin and started to accuse me of all sorts of revolutions and things. I nearly wet my pants at first, thinking they were sending me back to the States as a petty thief. Then I saw they were, damn it, *afraid* of me! I mean, they kept acting like I was about to spring at them and eat them up and, damn it, it felt *good*."

Captain Gringo laughed incredulously and asked, "You enjoyed playing the role, like an actor?"

"Yeah. And I fooled the shit out of them, too. I knew I was getting in deeper and deeper by the minute, but I just couldn't stop. I didn't know *how* to stop. You see, I've played at being a banker and I've played at being a journalist, but I never had a chance to be a notorious soldier of fortune. You understand, right?"

"Wrong. That's the craziest story I've ever heard, and you tell some pissers. Did you really steal that money in the States, or did you make that up, too?"

Porter sighed and said, "Oh, I really fiddled with the books. But as a matter of fact it does sound better when I say I stole a whole lot. I've met some really wild guys since I've been on the dodge and I wouldn't want them to think I was a sissy."

Captain Gringo shook his head and said, "I noticed you've learned to pick locks. Let me show you how to clean a machine gun. The first thing we do is drain the water jacket and get the damned thing off."

Porter stood up to join him at the workbench. Then he said, "I just thought of a great way for this adventure to end. You see, we get to this jungle cove and there's a lost white gal living there, raised by the natives to be their queen."

"For Chrissake, knock it off, Bill. We're not having an adventure. We're running for our fucking lives. Real life doesn't work out so neatly. Sometimes I don't think God likes happy endings."

Porter sighed and said, "I know. He's got a lousy sense of humor, too. If I was God, everybody would have a more interesting life with lots of laughs and a few neat twists to keep them on their toes."

"Well, you're not God and I don't know how we're going to get out of this mess, either. Take off that jacket and roll up your sleeves. Maybe you'll find something funny to write someday about cleaning guns. I've always found it boring as hell, but it has to be done."

5

They were over two hundred miles from the Gulf of Darien as the crow flies, but *La Tortuga* was not a crow. She had salt in her condensers and the bulge of Eastern Panama was in the way. So Captain Gringo took the helm well before the sun could catch them on the open sea and swung in toward the shore. Gaston had been down in the engine room, swearing at everyone. So he was surprised by the new compass heading when he rejoined his friend and a navy deserter called Quico in the wheelhouse of the conning tower. He stared out across the inky water as the sky began to pearl more stars away and said, "I hope you don't think this is rude of me, Dick, but you are steaming south."

Captain Gringo said, "I know. We've rounded Point San Blas and the charts say there's an archipelago of off-shore keys we can run behind."

Gaston said, "Las Mulatas. I find it most fatiguing to keep reminding you that you are crazy."

"You know the islands, Gaston?"

"Of course not. I'm a white man. Las Mulatas and the reefs around them are charted by guess and by God. Every mariner with any sense avoids them."

Captain Gringo nodded and said, "I noticed that on the charts. I doubt like hell that we'll meet a British cruiser in waters charted as shoal. I sure wish we had a radio man aboard. By now they must be gossiping like hell

49

about us and it would help if we knew where they thought we were."

Gaston said, "You are needed here, to doubtless run us on a reef. I have been nursing the condensers with some very ordinary wine. I don't know who else might be able to read Morse."

Captain Gringo frowned as he steered back on his heading after an unexpected swell had yawed them slightly. He said, "I have to get some sleep. I could swear I just heard you say you'd been drinking with the condensers."

Gaston said, *"Merde alors,* I would never submit my poor liver to the Madeira I found in the ship's stores. They have, or had, barrels of the swill. It had all gone from bad to worse. It is not true that Madeira is improved by a long sea voyage. It is swill to begin with and it just keeps getting worse. But it may help, in the boiler water."

"Back up and say that again. You fed *wine* into our *engines?*"

"Mon Dieu, you may call it wine. I call it vinegar. The acid will do little to cut the salt encrustations building up in our condenser tubes but if there is any lime . . ."

"Oh, I get it," Captain Gringo cut in, remembering his high school chemistry. He laughed and added, "Leave it to a Frenchman to know every angle when it comes to wine. You're crazy, too, but I can see how it just might work. The acetic acid in sour wine should dissolve calcium, magnesium, and most other salts. How far do you think we can steam on your weird boiler water?"

Gaston shrugged and replied, "What does it matter? We should run aground any minute. Regard those swells out there. Even as an old army man I can tell you the water is shallow and getting more so as you persist in this madness."

Captain Gringo turned to Quico and raised an eyebrow. The sailor nodded and said, "Señor Gaston is right. *La Tortuga* is a shallow draft gunboat, but one needs *some* water under her keel. Before I got in trouble with the navy I used to stand watch at the helm, as I told you before. I was only a yeoman, but one hears the officers talking on the bridge, even though nobody is supposed to talk on the bridge."

"So talk and get to the point, Quico."

"I heard the officers speak of these Mulatas. They are not called mules because they are half black and half white. They are called mules because they are half land and half sea. Islands that the charts show above the water may be under it. Shoals on the maps are inclined to become islands when the tide goes out. But that is not all. The officers said Las Mulatas move sideways on the charts. There are reefs and islands where the map says they are not supposed to be. I think that when they mapped these waters, long ago, somebody must have been very very drunk. Or maybe the currents have moved the sands over the years."

Gaston said, "Give it up, Dick. We'll be a duck on the water for any gunboat that finds us hard aground and miles from any shore!"

Captain Gringo put a hand on the engine room telegraph and moved the indicator to dead slow, but maintained his course as he saw the horizon line was smudged by palms. The vessel began to rock more as they lost steerageway, but he said, "It's getting light enough to see breakers ahead. We'll get that key over there between us and the open sea before we drop anchor and figure out where the hell we are."

Before anyone could argue, the lookout on the mast above them called down, "Smoke astern!" and Captain Gringo snapped, "Quico, take the wheel!" Then, as the sailor did so, he and Gaston ran out on the wing to peer back along their wake. The sky to the north was purple-gray. The rising sun, though still below the horizon, was catching a distant smoke plume in its web of gold. Gaston swore and said, "If we can see their smoke, they can see ours, *non?*"

Captain Gringo said, "No bet. It could be just a passing freighter. Run into the radio shack and see if you can pick anything up."

Gaston nodded and left. The tall American stood alone on the wing, watching. He couldn't tell if the other vessel was headed their way or not. The distance was too great and their relative speeds were too slow. If they could keep it that way, things might improve. Once the sun was up, the smoke plumes would be less visible against the sky. But they'd still be visible.

He ducked inside, took the helm, and told Quico, "Run down to the engine room. Tell them to douse the fires."

"Don't you mean *bank* the fires, Señor?"

"No. I want them completely out. We're burning oil, not coal. We can turn the jets back on at a moment's notice. Meanwhile we still have enough pressure to make that key over there."

Quico grinned in understanding, saluted, and left. The American at the helm knew he was being observed from the other vessel, whether it was an innocent freighter or a warship. So he swung the wheel hard aport and while there was still time, set a course at right angles to where he really intended to go. When his smoke plume faded out, they'd have a false bearing on his course and, what the hell, they painted these tubs horizon gray to make them hard to see.

Bill Porter came up to join him. Porter was not alone. The rebel girl who'd loaned him her hairpin was with Porter. In the confusion up to now, Captain Gringo hadn't noticed she was gorgeous. Porter said, "Dick, this is Señorita O'Hara. I told her you knew where we were going."

The girl said, "I am called Catalina Lopez O'Hara y Batista. The others have appointed me to talk because I speak English."

Captain Gringo said, "I noticed the Irish eyes, but your brogue is still Spanish. What can I do for you, Cathy?"

"You might tell us where we are. Some of my people think we are off Las Mulatas and this worries them."

He smiled thinly down at her and said, "They're right. It worries me, too. We're nursing a cranky engine and there's a strange vessel off our stern. My friend, Gaston, is trying to pick up any wireless signals they're sending about us."

Porter looked surprised and said, "Oh, do we have a wireless set aboard?" and Captain Gringo said, "Yes. Unfortunately only Gaston and me read Morse. I'd rather have him on the after guns, but we've only got one Gaston."

Porter said, "I used to work as a telegrapher. I'm not sure how these Marconi things work, but I can take down Morse."

"In Spanish?"

"I guess so. As well as I can speak it, which isn't saying much."

Captain Gringo said, "It's better than nothing. Go through that door and turn right. Tell Gaston to get you set up as our new Sparks and report back to me, pronto."

Porter nodded and moved off with surprising grace for such a beefy man. Captain Gringo had enough distractions without a pretty little Spanish-Irish *muchachita* on the bridge, but he couldn't think of a friendly way to tell her to beat it, so he didn't.

He'd hardly had time to get to know his hastily improvised crew or his passengers. It seemed unusual for Hispanics to appoint a female go-between, but he didn't want to argue the point. So when Catalina asked if there was anything she could do to help he said, "Run out on the port wing and con that smoke plume behind us from time to time."

"Port wing? Con?"

"That little balcony outside the left hand door is the wing. I want you to see if you can tell if the ship over to the northeast is just passing or if it's following us."

She brightened and literally dashed outside. He noticed she moved like a dancer and as he glanced out at her from time to time he saw the rising sun was picking up copper highlights in her otherwise black hair. Catalina was suntanned more than most high-toned Hispanic women thought proper, but there was a pale line of creamier flesh along the low collar line of her pleated peasant blouse. He swung his gaze to more important and less interesting views as he felt the vessel losing way under him. The damned fools in the engine room had killed the fires without cracking the throttles wider. He signaled for half speed. He wouldn't get it, with the engines running on the slowly dying pressure in the still-hot boilers, but the key he had in mind was aft his starboard beam, now, and, knowing that no smoke was indicating his course at the moment, he swung the wheel hard over and watched his gray steel bow sweep south. The twin barrels of the forward turret were trained almost on the palm-covered island as he made for it. The vessel was slowing by the minute, but *La Tortuga* had a lot of mass for her size and she could probably coast a couple of miles under no power at all, if you were satisfied with slow as hell.

Catalina came back inside and said, "I can't tell if that other ship is moving or not. There is no wind. The smoke just seems to hang there."

He said, "Don't look for a minute or so. You have a mental picture of it, now. The next time you duck out you'll be able to judge whether it's closer or farther away."

She nodded and joined him at the wheel. She studied his profile as he stared ahead. She said, "I didn't know you were an admiral, too. Jesus Gomez tells us you served with Balboa Brigade in the last Panamanian revolution."

He shrugged and said, "I led what was left of the Balboas out. Who are you people?"

"Gomez is a Balboa. Most of us are Republicanos."

"No kidding? The last time I was through, your outfits were as busy killing each other as you were the Colombian occupation forces."

She nodded and said, "I know. That is why Bogota still runs the isthmus from the highlands. But all Panamanian patriots have agreed to work together. Some of your North American friends have been arming and funding us for a proper revolution."

He grimaced and said, "I don't have many North American friends these days. I'm not too sure *you* do, either. You know, of course, that you're being used?"

Catalina laughed lightly and replied, "Of course. That is the way of this world. *El Pulpo del Norte* wishes a free Panama in order for them to finish the canal the French started. When they are not telling us how much they wish for us to be free, they call us 'Greasers'."

"How do you feel about that, Cathy?"

"How should one feel? I have not had a bath since they arrested me and the others, but I don't think I am any greasier than anyone else would be under the circumstances. Let them call us what they like, as long as they send money and arms. Let them build their canal. Some day it will be ours. The important thing is the liberation of my country. Colombia had no reason to claim our isthmus when they broke free from Spain. We Panamanians had been here as long as anyone. The city of Panama was settled before the city of Bogota. We did not wish for to get rid of Spanish masters in order to have Colombian masters. Why do you suppose the Colombians won't let us go? They never come down here. They send their military and officials, but the rich Bogota politicos prefer to live up there in their mountains. It is most stupid as well as unjust. Why fight to keep land you don't want?"

He didn't answer until he saw that last ground swell wasn't going to put them on the bottom plates after all. Then he said, "People are like that. It's called Pink Map Fever. Queen Victoria has the worst case, in this century, but it seems to be catching."

"Pink Map Fever? I don't understand, Captain Gringo."

"Call me Dick, Cathy. I don't understand it, either. Old Queen Vickie hardly ever travels and God knows she's rich, but she has all sorts of people out painting the map pink for her. British explorers have died like flies all over the world trying to name some backwoods waterfall or mountain after her. They shoot a bunch of fuzzy-wuzzy people who never saw a pair of shoes before and tell them they're now British subjects. Everybody else seems to feel the same way. The new young Kaiser has guys out claiming any parts the British missed and now he owns barren deserts bigger than all of Germany, on the map. They seem to be using the world for a game board. The winner is the one with the most square inches painted his or her color."

The girl sighed and said, "We don't want to be Colombia's color. We don't want to be painted yellow, like other Americano possessions, either. Your own country has this fever, no?"

"I told you it was catching. To be fair to Bogota, they probably think somebody is trying to take away some inches on their map. The isthmus was transferred direct from Spain to them when they signed the final treaties a while back, remember?"

She replied, "How could I remember? I am only nineteen. The point is that the past is dead and Panama has no future as a neglected province of Colombia. They are not interested in anything but collecting taxes from us. Bogota gives nothing to us for our tax money. Is this just?"

"No. It's the way most governments see things, Cathy."

"It is strange you call me that, Deek. My name is Catalina, but my grandfather called me Cathy when I was little."

"Grandpa was the Irishman in your family tree, right?"

"*Si,* he was a famous rebel against the English. They were sending him to Australia in chains, but he got away."

"Seems to run in the family, eh? What are you going to do after you win your independence from Colombia, Cathy?"

"Oh, we will live happily ever after, I suppose. But victory seems far away at the moment, and you seem to be taking us even farther. You have still not told me where we are going, Deek."

The wheel shuddered in his hands as the rudder hit something he sincerely hoped was soft coral. The key he was hoping to shelter behind was closer, now. He didn't see any signs of human habitation under the palms or among the rank underbrush. There were no mangroves on this side. That meant the water was at least five or six feet deep just off the coral beaches. He wondered how much water *La Tortuga* drew. She wasn't a Mississippi steamboat. She was an ocean-going vessel. The waters the rising sun was revealing were too green and silty to qualify as ocean.

He knew Cathy was waiting for some reassurance, so he said, "First things first. We got you and your friends out of those chains and Bogota isn't going to get to hang you after all."

"We are most indebted to you for that, Deek. But

56

now that we are free and armed again, where are we *going?*"

"You see that little island just ahead? That's where we're going at the moment. Run out and see if that other vessel is still ghosting us."

She shrugged, ran out on the bridge, then came back and said, "It is not as close. Why are we going to that island? Nobody lives on Las Mulatas."

"I sure hope you're right. The guys we took this gunboat away from ran a sloppy show, which was sort of fortunate for us in one way. But they were careless about their boiler water, which is not so good. I suppose when they topped their feed water in some lagoon they just tasted to see if it was fresh enough. A man can drink water with a little salt in it. A steam engine can't. We have to drain our boilers and flush them out with fresh water."

"But everyone knows there is no fresh water on Las Mulatas, Deek."

"I wish you hadn't said that."

Before they could get deeper into the water they might or might not find ashore, Gaston came in, saying, *"M'sieu* Porter knows as much as I do about these mysterious Marconi waves. That other ship either has no wireless or it does not see fit to use it. We picked up some most distant dots and dashes, but the signal fades in and out. Neither of us could make the message out."

Captain Gringo introduced Gaston and Catalina to each other and said, "That other smoke plume seems to be fading away, too. But we're not out of the woods yet. Have you checked the fore and aft gun turrets, Gaston?"

The Frenchman nodded and said, "There are no mice in either, but little more can be said for them. I opened the breechblocks and there would seem to be no birds' nests built in any of the barrels, but the rust, ooh, la! la!"

"We know the former crew had a casual attitude. What about ammo?"

Gaston shrugged and said, "Full racks of British Armstrong four-inch shells. One would gather they didn't hold target practice often. The shell casings are a lovely shade of green. I would say they came with the original paint job." He chuckled and added, "I don't think this tub has been repainted since they got it from the Royal Navy."

Captain Gringo grimaced and said, "The detonating caps are as old, then. What are the odds if we have to fire at anyone?"

"Fifty-fifty, I hope. Who are we about to fire on, Dick?"

"Anybody we have to," growled Captain Gringo. He turned to Cathy and asked, "Do any of your guerrillas have any artillery experience, Cathy?"

The girl replied, "I think Jesus Gomez might. He was in your old Balboa Brigade, remember?"

The tall American swore under his breath and said, "I remember. He couldn't hit the broad side of a barn with a rifle. You'd better check the navy deserters, Gaston. One of them could be a gunner's mate or something."

Gaston said, *"Merde,* I will go with *something.* How would one expect to find a gunner's mate in a navy that allows its guns to rust?"

"Ask around anyhow. Useless soldiers and sailors desert good armies and navies. Maybe it works in reverse with a lousy navy. Old Quico's not a bad helmsman. He says he took off because they never promoted anyone on merit and tended to bully guys from poor families."

Gaston sighed, "Ever the optimist. I shall inquire among the deserters. But have you ever met a deserter who admitted he was simply a useless camel who couldn't carry his load?"

Cathy had been listening, of course. She said. "They kept us separated from their navy prisoners. But I can tell you the Bogota government is a tight oligarchy and that they give all the good jobs to relatives. That is one of the main reasons we Panamanians wish for to be free."

"To give the good jobs to your own relatives?" smiled Gaston.

The girl's eyes blazed as she spat back, "Of course not. Panama will be a *true* democracy. Wait and see."

The last thing Captain Gringo felt like listening to was a political argument between a cynic and a dedicated militant. So he shot Gaston a warning frown and said, "You'd better go forward and man that brace of bow guns. Pick up some help if you can. Play it by ear if you can't. We're almost in range of that island."

Gaston glanced through the windscreen and asked, "How can you tell? We're hardly moving. But never mind. I shall leave you love birds alone as I prepare to do battle with coconut trees."

Gaston left and Cathy asked, "Why did he say that? Did you tell him we were lovers?"

"No. He's French. Don't worry about your reputation, Cathy. Everyone aboard knows we just met and haven't been alone together."

She said, "That is true. We are alone, now, but not even French people could be expected to make love in such a functional place, even if it was private. But you must understand that gossip is second only to cockfighting as a national sport. That other girl with me swears she is pure, but she has a terrible reputation. Under ordinary circumstances I would not associate with Cielita, but revolution makes strange bedfellows."

Captain Gringo said, "So I've noticed," as the wheel started going mushy in his hands. They were drifting with a westbound current he hadn't felt up to now. He cranked the telegraph to full speed to see if there was enough pressure left to gain some steerageway. He said, "You'd better take another peek at the other steamer's smoke, now," so Cathy ducked out on the wing. The deck began to vibrate under his boots and he saw the engine was still breathing, but not too hard. The wheel began to steady as the screws kicked more water back against the rudders. The island was quite close, now, and the sun was high enough for him to make out coconuts in the palm tops. That was a hopeful sign. The trees were lousy with nuts. Ergo, nobody was harvesting them.

Who the hell was Cielita? He'd paid little attention to either of the girls they'd rescued. He hadn't noticed Cathy was pretty until just now. They'd both been dirty and sort of messy when they'd come out of the brig. He'd noticed one was white and the other a *mestiza* when he let them out. Period. He'd been more worried about securing

59

the ship at the time than what a couple of teary-eyed dames looked like.

Quico rejoined him on the bridge to report, "That is the end of the steam, Captain. The man you made engineer says to tell you the screws are barely moving, even at full steam. He says if we do not start the fires again we will be dead in the water within minutes."

"Do you think he knows what he's talking about, Quico?"

"*Quien sabe?* He used to be an oiler on a coastal freighter before they drafted him. Have you any further orders, Captain?"

"Yeah. You just made Third Mate. How do you feel about a man on the bow with a lead line? We've just enough momentum to make it to the lee of that key. But I'd sure hate to hit a reef, about now."

Quico said, "I mean no disrespect, Captain, but it is too late to worry about a bow man. The lookout above us will see any big shoal in any case. But what can you do if he does?"

"Hmm, you're right. Reversing screws without power would be useless. We're just going to have to trust to luck. But, what the hell, the island's almost abeam."

As they half moved and half drifted around the end of the island he could see other islands beyond it. Some were only a mile or so off, others further. The horizon was an unbroken line of misty purple palm and mangrove, maybe five miles away. He could see they were among the notorious Mulatas. There was no landmark telling him just where. But he'd study the charts later. Once they were anchored out of sight. If they *could* anchor out of sight.

Cathy came back in. She said, "The smoke is still there. I can't tell if it's closer or farther away. The sun is making for confusion."

He said, "Quico, take the helm. If the rudders respond at all, we're trying to swing behind the palms, right?"

"I understand, my Captain."

Captain Gringo led Cathy back out on the port wing. The sun was low in the east. The open sea was hazed by morning fog lying like a shag rug under a clear cobalt-blue

60

sky. He couldn't make out the hull of the distant steamer to the northwest. But its smoke was still a watery ink blot above the distant horizon. He told the girl, "They seem to be just standing off, there. They may have anchored. The water's shallow enough a hundred miles out."

Cathy asked, "Why would anyone stop out there in the middle of nowhere, Deek?"

He said, "I don't know everything. I just like to tell people I do. They may be watching us. They may be fishing. They may be smugglers waiting to meet somebody."

"Why are they not as clever as we about their smoke, Deek?"

"They obviously want to keep their steam, in case they have to move someplace in a hurry."

She squinted at the mysterious smoke plume and said, "If they are the navy, why don't they attack?"

"People don't attack an armored gunboat with four-inchers lightly. Let's see if they're talking about us."

They went back inside. He glanced out the windscreen, saw they were rounding the end of the desert island, and told Quico, "You're doing fine. Steady as she goes. We'll be in the radio shack if you need us."

They moved aft to find Bill Porter seated at a table with a pair of earphones on his head. Porter didn't notice them until Captain Gringo patted his shoulder and asked, loudly, "How are we doing, Bill?"

Porter jumped half out of his skin before he saw who it was. He took off the headset and said, "This is kind of interesting. I just had a great idea for a story. How far can you send these Marconi waves, Dick?"

"I think the signal's good for twenty miles or more. Why?"

"Oh, heck, I had this plot where a guy in Europe is sending advance stock market news to a confederate on Wall Street and . . ."

"Never mind the fantasy, damn it. Is anybody in the real world signaling our position?"

Porter said, "No. I think a British warship is talking to a Dutchman about a storm warning. But they must be way the hell off. The sky out there is clear as far as you can see. If that spooky steamer out there has a set of sparks they don't seem to be using it. But hardly anybody has wireless, anyway."

Captain Gringo frowned and filled Porter in on the little he knew about the smoke on the horizon. Porter said, "I'll bet they're pirates."

Captain Gringo sighed and said, "I figured you would. There aren't any pirates anymore, Bill. We're going back to the helm. Give a yell if you hear from Blackbeard or Morgan."

They'd just reached the wheelhouse when all hell broke loose. Captain Gringo yelled, "Down!" and shoved Cathy to the deck as the glass all around was sharded by automatic fire! It sounded like two machine guns or an old Gatling was bouncing lead off the conning tower. As he dropped to his own hands and knees and started crawling toward the helm, Captain Gringo saw that Quico was on his back and covered with blood and broken glass, the wheel was spinning wildly with no hands to hold it, and *La Tortuga* was yawning to starboard as if she wanted to crawl up on the beach and lay some eggs.

Captain Gringo grabbed the spokes of the wheel, still on the floor, as another burst of slugs sheeted through the shattered windscreen and pocked paint off the steel bulkhead over Cathy's screaming head. He steadied the helm, but had no idea where the hell he was steering from down here by Quico's corpse. Then the keel bit into coral with a long low groan that tingled the whole vessel like a giant dentist's drill and they weren't going anywhere. They were hard aground, and bullets were still bouncing off their plates.

The deck jolted under him as a big gun went off. He sincerely hoped it was one of their own. He told Cathy, "Crawl back to the radio shack and tell Porter to flatten out, too. This is no place for a lady and it could make a gentleman nervous, too. I'll try to work my way to Gaston, forward. Don't stick your heads out until I tell you to."

Cathy had obviously had some practice with guns and she started crawling on her hands and knees from the wheelhouse. He had to follow in the same position at least as far as the first interior ladder, so a disinterested observer might have thought they looked like sniffing dogs.

They split up at the ladder well and he slid down three levels to move forward along the companionway running the length of the vessel under the steel main deck. A naked lady ran out of a compartment, yelling that she was being murdered in her bed. It was the other rebel girl, Cielita, and she wasn't in her bed, but trying to climb him like a ladder for some reason. He steadied her, trying to keep his hands polite as they encountered sweaty naked female flesh no matter where he put them. Cielita was hysterical. So he shook her and snapped, "Get back to your cabin and put some clothes on. We're aground and under fire, but there's plenty of armor plate between you and whoever in hell is making all that noise."

She didn't move her feet, but she tried to kiss him as she sobbed something about being a good girl. He could see how good she'd be. But this was neither the time nor the place. So he scooped her up and carried her through the hatchway she'd popped out of. He saw that she and, he hoped, Cathy had been sharing an officer's cabin under the tower.

He dumped her on the rumpled bed under the overhead lamp in the portless compartment. Cielita looked up coyly and said, "Don't leave me. I am most frightened."

Then she gasped as she stared past his head at the light bulb above them and said, "Oh, the light is going out, Señor!"

He said, "Yeah, the generator's running out of steam, too. I've got to go, Cielito. Here, take these matches. Get dressed and wait here until someone comes for you. I don't want you running around in a fire fight, with or without your clothes on."

"Please don't leave me alone. I will give myself to you if only you will stay!"

"Another time." He sighed, ducking out the hatchway. The bulbs along the overhead were a dull orange glow, now, and he cursed himself for giving his matches to the idiotic girl when they winked off and left him in total darkness. He started groping his way forward with

63

his left hand on a brass rail and when he banged into a ladder he looked up and saw a dim gray blur of daylight somewhere above. He yelled out, "Is that the forward turret up there?" and was relieved to hear Gaston reply, "Is that you, Dick? *Merde alors,* I thought they blew you off the conning tower!"

Captain Gringo went up the ladder to join Gaston and two sailors in the cramped confines of the pillbox-shaped fore turret. Gaston spit on the smoking breech of the starboard gun and said, "This triple-titted son of a toad has a shell up her ass and won't give it back."

"I just heard you get one round off. What the fuck is going on?"

"Mon Dieu, don't *you* know, either? Whoever they were, they would seem to be leaving."

Captain Gringo stepped over to the aiming slit and squinted out. A schooner with all sails reefed was showing them her stern as she moved off under power, going too fast to be reasonable. He said, "They're out of range. But they sure gave us a dusting. We're aground and Quico's dead. They must have been skulking in the lee of the island and they didn't spot us coming because we'd killed our smoke."

Gaston said, *"Merde,* tell me something I didn't know. The camels opened up on us on sight. One would assume they have a guilty conscience about something. They doubtless took us for a government patrol boat."

The mysterious schooner was moving to put another little clump of coral and coconut between them. Captain Gringo said, "It's a good thing they were only armed with small-bore stuff. Things are starting to fall in place. She was waiting here to make contact with that other vessel offshore. They must be smugglers or gun runners. You think *they* scared *us?* They must have shit, when the bow of a gunboat popped around the corner at them!"

"Oui. They had no way of knowing most of our shells are corroded. I sped them on their way with a very near miss, if I say so myself. I'd have blown them out of the water if this species of insect would perform like a real four-incher. But how can they *move* like that, Dick? They

showed no smoke, either. But they are most certainly not steaming like that under reserve pressure!"

The tall American said, "I'll bet they have one of those new diesel engines. I didn't understand what all the fuss was about when that German took out his patent back in '92. I figured an engine was just an engine, but look at that little bugger go! That steamer out to sea must be the mother ship, and they're using the sneaky schooner for whatever it is they have in mind close in."

"Perhaps. But why have a mother ship at all? The schooner we just fought is big enough to go anywhere under her own power, *non?*"

"You're right. The bigger one may be carrying fuel for its pump. More likely, it has the hold space to carry something its pump was waiting to deliver. You remember those San Blas Indians we met up with along this coast a while back?"

"Ah, who could forget La Blanca and her bare derriere."

"She wore a mess of pearls, too. One of the things that makes the San Blas so truculent is that people keep trying to take their pearls and pearl beds away from them. If those guys on the schooner are pearl pirates . . ."

"Stop right there. There are not enough pearls in the entire world to require the services of a steam freighter, Dick. You could load a king's ransom in that schooner's lockers."

Captain Gringo said, "You're as bad as Bill Porter, in your own way. He keeps dreaming up fantastic ideas. You bust every bubble you see. I've got to inspect the damages and see if we can get off this reef. You coming, Pollyanna?"

Gaston said, *"Mais non,* I have to get these guns in order and show these men how to properly man a turret. Let me know if we seem to be sinking."

Captain Gringo left Gaston and his crew to do what they could about the neglected gear. It only took him a few minutes to find out that nobody had been hurt but the late Quico. The gunners on the other vessel had thrown most of their fire at the conning tower. He knew he'd have done the same. Ergo, whoever they were and whatever they were up to, they were pros.

He sent a runner to the engine room to tell them to relight the oil burners. He was pretty sure the others weren't attached to any recognized navy. They'd have signaled before opening fire on a strange gunboat if they'd had a proper hunting license for these waters.

He found Cathy still with Bill Porter in the radio shack. Porter was in his seat and trying to pick up wireless signals, so he wasn't totally useless. But the other American reported that the airways were clear.

Captain Gringo noticed Cathy followed him back to the bridge. As he stepped out on the wing for a look-see, Cathy knelt and gently closed the dead Quico's eyes. She said something about a Christian burial as he came back in. He said, "We'll bury him on shore in a while. But first things first. We have to find out if we can *go* ashore."

He moved the engine room telegraph to full astern, in case anything still worked. Then he said, "Steam's building up. That other vessel is moving off. They must have heard our gunfire across the water."

As he moved back to take the helm the screws were starting to turn over and the deck shuddered under them. He said, "I think we can back off. Then we'll move alee the right way and I'll take a shore party in behind a machine gun."

Cathy asked, "Do you think some of those banditos may still be on the island, Deek?"

He grinned wolfishly and said, "I sure hope so. They owe us for what they did to Quico and our paint job."

6

They got behind the island and anchored a rifle shot off-shore. They pointed both gun turrets at the trees and underbrush in case anybody wanted to make something out of it.

Apparently nobody did. So Captain Gringo left Gaston in charge of *La Tortuga* as he led a shore party in. He took the machine gun and Bill Porter along with Jesus Gomez and a mixed squad of rebels and deserters. Porter said he didn't know anything about patroling. Captain Gringo said it was time he learned. Actually, he wanted at least one good-sized guy who spoke English along. He felt Gomez could be trusted not to stab him in the back, but Gomez had not been an impressive fighter in the old Balboa Brigade. These new rebels and deserters from the Colombian Navy didn't know each other well enough to have started the usual plots against a blue-eyed commander. So they'd probably follow orders for now. But he'd noticed a few sullen looks and a sluggish obedience in certain quarters since he'd let the whole bunch out of the brig. Somebody was putting bugs in their ears. Things were going too well. Latins didn't like to take orders from anyone, if they could help it, and taking orders from a gringo really seemed to piss them off. The only guerrilla outfits he'd ever led without a lot of bullshit from the ranks had been under fire from superior forces. More than one son of a bitch among this new bunch probably thought he was as good a gunboat skipper as the next guy.

They rowed ashore. Gomez leaped out with the painter and pulled the bow aground in the quiet water. Captain Gringo braced the Maxim in the bow and told Gomez, "Take your three rebels to the tree line while I cover you."

Gomez nodded and raised his rifle to port arms. But one of the men with him asked, "For why do *we* have to take all the chances while you and these sailors stay here?"

Captain Gringo dredged the man's name from his busy memory and said, "Because I told you to, Moreno."

Gomez said, "Idiot! Can't you see he is covering our advance with a machine gun? He must stay here for to point the gun at the trees. The sailors must stay here for to get us off in a hurry should we have to fall back."

Moreno shrugged and didn't answer. But he followed, grudgingly, as Gomez led him and the others toward the green wall of leaves. Porter moved up beside his fellow American and asked, "Do you always get an argument like that?"

"They'll shake down in a day or so. What do you know about automatic weapons, Bill?"

"Not a fucking thing."

"Good. You don't have any mistaken ideas to get rid of. You see how this ammo belt rises in folds from that box on the duckboards? If I have to fire, I want you to make sure the belt doesn't kink as it feeds. If you see me getting to the end of a belt, haul that other box in place. You can see how it opens. Just grab the end of the belt and hand it to me when I reach out. Okay?"

"I'll try. How many bullets do you figure you'll need, for God's sake?"

"None, or a lot. These things fire six hundred rounds a minute and there's only a hundred or so in each belt. One of the popular misconceptions I don't have to explain to *you* in detail is that these new guns are not the final argument. You saw back there on the gunboat that you can throw a lot of lead without hitting enough to matter. They got one of us. But they fired more bullets than Custer caught at Little Big Horn and didn't even bust our light bulbs. You can get in trouble overestimating these things. One rifle is worth more than a machine gun, if it's aimed by an expert and the machine gunner is just hosing the garden."

Porter nodded and said, "I can see why your machine gun skills are in demand down here. What was that stuff Gaston was saying about the slugs he picked off the wheelhouse floor? Can you really tell what kind of a machine gun those guys on the schooner had, just by looking at the mashed-up lead?"

Captain Gringo nodded and said, "Yeah, the spent rounds were unjacketed .45s like the U.S. Army just phased out. We figure they fired an old Gatling gun at us. There are hundreds of them around on the international market. I heard some Chinese warlords have them, these days." Porter looked relieved and said, "That's a break. I thought those other rascals had a real machine gun!"

Captain Gringo looked disgusted and said, "A Gatling *is* a real machine gun, in case you weren't listening when they shot out all the windows."

"Oh, sure, a Gatling's rapid fire, but it's not *modern,* is it?"

Captain Gringo saw Gomez waving at him. He picked the Maxim off its mounts and said, "Lug those ammo boxes, will you, Bill?" Then, in Spanish, he told the men in the launch to stay put as he swung his legs over the side to wade ashore. As they trudged up the beach toward Gomez and the others, he told Porter, "The only advantage of these so-called modern machine guns is that they're lighter. The guys on the schooner can throw a little *more* lead, as a matter of fact. The Gatling is a good gun. It's just too heavy since battle tactics have changed since the Civil War. I'd take a Gatling over a Maxim in an old-fashioned Waterloo against regimental squares. But they didn't work out against Apache very good. Apache won't line up and advance across an open field with fixed bayonets and it's sort of hard to haul a Gatling over a mountain, so. . ."

"I get the picture," Porter cut in. Then he shot a nervous glance back at the boat and murmured, "Aren't we taking a chance, leaving those guys back there? What if they decide to haul ass and strand us here?"

Captain Gringo said, "They can't. Gaston is covering

them with four-inchers and there's no place but *La Tortuga* to punk out to. Have you been picking up the dirty looks and whispers, too?"

Porter said, "Well, some of them seem a little resentful. I think it's because the three of us seem to have taken over. My Spanish isn't so hot, but I overheard a couple of them saying something about electing a leader."

"I imagine you did. That's the trouble with fighting for democracy. There's always some asshole who thinks you can run an army by voice vote. We'll worry about that later."

They joined Gomez and his scouts. Gomez pointed into the brush and said, "There seems to be nobody living here, my Captain. I can see the sea on the other side of the trees. Maybe if you swept with that Maxim we would know for certain that no *pobrecitos* were hiding from us under a bush, no?"

Captain Gringo shook his head and said, "Let's do it the hard way. Any Indians or castaways on this key are obviously more scared than full of fight."

He lowered the Maxim to a fallen log and said, "Put the ammo boxes down here, Bill. I'll take the point."

Porter waited until Captain Gringo had drawn his revolver and was moving under the trees before he fell in beside him and asked, "How come we abandoned the machine gun, Dick?"

"We didn't abandon it. We'll pick it up on the way back to the launch. Look at this fucking brush all around us. This is hit-and-run country, Bill. If you get off one round at a target of opportunity you're doing good."

"Oh, I see. You figure a heavy weapon would just be clumsy in under these trees, right?"

"You're learning. I think you really must want to write a book. Pipe down and keep your eyes and ears open. I'll lecture you on scouting and patroling after we make sure nobody else on this key is better at it than me."

So they swept the island from one end to the other. As he'd suspected from the abundance of coconuts, the key was uninhabited. The nuts hung from every tree and littered the coral sand all around. Here and there one had sprouted. But most of the older nuts were rotting in the heavy shade of the overhead palm fans or the bushes they'd fallen into. Bill Porter spotted some fruit on a lush green bush and started to reach for an "apple". But Captain Gringo hauled him back before his fingers could make contact and snapped, "Jesus H. Christ! How long have you been down here?"

"About six months. Why? Aren't those apples any good?"

"That's not an apple tree. It's a manacheel."

"Gee, it sure *looks* like an apple tree, Dick."

"I know. I think the first sucker who picked one was with Columbus. The fruit are poisonous, which seems reasonable enough. The leaves make poison ivy look like a sissy. The whole damned plant thinks it's a cobra. Men have died or gone blind from the smoke, trying to burn a manacheel out. Stay the hell away from any weed you haven't been formally introduced to. I've got enough to worry about."

"Can I touch those coconuts? They *are* coconuts, aren't they?"

"Yeah. But don't mess with them either. The milk in the old windfalls is stronger than beer, and green coconut meat can give you the shits. What's wrong with you? Didn't you eat breakfast?"

By now they'd secured the area, so Captain Gringo led his little patrol back to where they'd left the Maxim, retrieved it, and moved down to the launch. He told the sailors they were alone on the island. Then he pointed to the tool chest in the stern and added, "You and you, break out some shovels and follow me. We're going to dig under the trees."

One of the men he'd indicated moved to obey him. The other sailor asked, "Why us? We rowed you ashore and we have for to row you back. Let one of these civilian *peones* do it. They are used to digging in the dirt."

Captain Gringo put the Maxim back on its mount in the bows before he straightened up, smiled pleasantly at the sullen sailor, and said, "Your mother sucks cock for *centavos*. Your sister sucks for free."

The sailor blanched and gasped, "Are you trying to provoke a fight, Señor?"

"Call me *Captain*, you self-abusing child of a one-titted whore. *You're* the one who seems to be looking for a fight! I didn't *ask* you to pick up that shovel. I *told* you to! Are you going to obey me or not?"

The sailor licked his lips and said, "You are not being just. You know I wear no pistol. If I reach for that rifle against the thwart you will have an excuse to kill me, no?"

"You learn fast, sailor. On the other hand, I don't think I'll shoot you if you go for that shovel. So it's your move."

The would-be-reluctant well digger took the shovel from the tool chest and climbed out to join his less mutinous comrade. Captain Gringo led the whole bunch back to the tree line, this time, and pointed out a low spot between some trees. The man who'd crossed him sunk the blade in and said, "I will dig, if you will take back what you said about the women of my family, Captain."

Captain Gringo nodded and said, "I never met the ladies, but I am sure they must all be saints."

Gomez followed Captain Gringo and Porter. When they sat on a fallen log, out of earshot from the others, Gomez said, "That big-mouth you just straightened out is not the one you have to worry about, my Captain. The open mouth only draws flies. It is the quiet man who puts the knife in your back."

The tall American nodded and said, "I've noticed that. We seem to be getting more than the usual resentment reserved for Anglos, though. Who's behind it, Gomez?"

Gomez shrugged and said, "I don't know. They stop talking when they notice me. They know we were in the Balboa Brigade together. You see, the Colombian police did not see fit to keep our bands intact when they rounded us up. The sailors are off different ships. The rebels you found me with came from at least three groups. We were working out our new chain of command when you rescued us."

Captain Gringo took out a smoke, lit up, and said, "Come on, you were on your way to trial and execution."

"*Es verdad*. That is why you have my undivided loyalty, my Captain! I remember you from the last revolution. Those other *pobrecitos* don't. There has been ugly talk about you and the women. One of them is said to be the woman of Angelo. I don't know which one of the women is his, but Angelo is the tall man with the scar on his cheek."

Captain Gringo swore under his breath and asked Porter if he was picking any of this up. Porter said, "Yeah, I get the picture. I'm an old Texas boy. The first thing I learned at my Daddy's knee was to leave Spanish gals alone. Why do you suppose they like to get us poor old Anglos in trouble, Dick?"

"I'm not sure. Hispanic men kill bulls to show everyone how pretty they are. Some of the girls seem to think it makes them look even prettier if a couple of idiots are fighting over them. Have you been messing with that gal you introduced me to?"

"Catalina? Lord, no, I know this makes me sound like a sissy, but I love my little wife, Athol. Catalina ain't bad, but she hasn't got my Athol's sweet smile. What made you ask a dumb question like that?"

Captain Gringo shrugged and said, "Gaston and me have been too busy to fool with either of the women since we grabbed *La Tortuga.* I'm trying to figure out how this Angelo got that fly between his horns."

Gomez said, "You were alone with Catalina for a time, were you not, my Captain?"

"Hell, I was alone with both of them, for that matter. But I haven't had time to ravage either of them, even if I was dumb enough."

"Es verdad, but Angelo is young, and not too bright, my Captain."

Captain Gringo blew a cloud of smoke and squinted into it to see if he could form an image of the one called Angelo. He had a vague picture of a good-looking squirt with a white knife-scar marring his big blue jaw. He hadn't paid much attention to Angelo because Angelo hadn't looked like the sort of hairpin you had to pay attention to. Angelo looked sort of dumb and hadn't much to say. He asked Gomez, "Were either of the girls in Angelo's rebel group when they were arrested?"

Gomez said, "I don't know. You see, before you and Señor Gaston let us out, there was mutual suspicion among the prisoners. It was the woman, Catalina, who suggested the military might have placed a spy among us. To tell the truth, the thought had not occurred to me until Catalina wondered aloud why they were taking us all to Bogota instead of just shooting us in Panama, as usual."

Porter said, "I noticed nobody but the girl wanted to talk to me when they tossed me in the clink. She was friendly. But, now that I think about it, she was pumping me."

Gomez said, "I will mingle among them and see if I can find out who told Angelo you were flirting with his woman, my Captain."

But the tall American said, "Forget it. They know you're Teacher's Pet. Anything you'll pick up will be a deliberate ruse. We'll just worry about getting our asses out of immediate danger as it comes up. If we find water, here, we should have no trouble making it to the Gulf of Darien. If we don't, a power struggle is academic."

Porter said, "I've been meaning to ask, Dick. What the hell's so hot about this Gulf of Darien you keep talking about?"

Captain Gringo said, "It'll be hot, all right. The point of getting there is that nobody important lives there anymore. We'll have time to figure out our futures without anyone shooting at us. These rebels and deserters can move either way after they've rested up and thought it out. They can work their way back to friends in Panama or head up into the Colombian highlands to dig for emeralds or start another revolution. You, Gaston, and me can make our own escape plans, once we beach *La Tortuga* and unload a mess of dependents."

He stood up and headed back to the well site as he heard one of the digging sailors shouting something. The others followed. When they got to the hole, it was to see the bottom was filled with pisscolored liquid. One of the sailors said, "I tasted it, Captain."

"You're a brave man. Is it fresh or saline?"

"A little of both, Captain. It is fresh enough for to nourish the roots of these coconut trees. It is fresh enough for to drink, if one holds one's nose. But for to put in a steam boiler, *quien sabe?*"

Captain Gringo swore softly and said, "Shit. Brackish won't do. We already have brackish boiler water. Unless

74

we can top it with pure fresh stuff. . . Never mind. We needed a grave for Quico, anyhow. Let's bring his body ashore and bury him."

He turned to head back to the launch. Porter fell in beside him to ask, "Can't we make it to that hideout in the gulf on the shit in our boilers, Dick?"

Captain Gringo said, "I don't know. We might make it. The valves may seize anywhere along the way and leave us wallowing dead in the water."

Porter grimaced and said, "Jesus, we'd be better off if we stayed here on shore, wouldn't we?"

"We can't stay here. That schooner may have gone to get help. That other vessel offshore might tell somebody we're here. Even if nobody comes to blast us off this key, we'd get sort of tired of . . . coconuts?"

Captain Gringo suddenly stopped, as if he'd taken root in the hot sand. He turned with a grin to stare up at the gently swaying palm fronds and said, "That's it. It's crazy, but I think it will work!"

Porter asked, "What are you talking about?" and Captain Gringo pointed at the trees and said, "Coconuts. Every one of them is full of *water*!"

Porter said, "You're right. It's crazy. I'm no expert, but I never heard of running a steam engine on coconut milk, for God's sake!"

But the soldier of fortune insisted, "Not coconut milk. Coconut water. The stuff they sell as milk is coconut meat grated up in the liquid of the nuts. There's a quart or so of almost pure water swishing around in a green nut, and those trees are lousy with nuts. There's a little oil emulsified in coconut water, but that's no problem. We feed oil into the steam for lubrication in any case. Let's get back to *La Tortuga* and tell the others."

Gomez had been listening. He said, "The idea sounds good, my Captain, but won't it mean an awful lot of work?"

"Yeah, we're going to have to tap a mess of nuts and it'll take all day or longer. But so what?"

"They are going to grumble, no?"

"Fuck 'em. Let 'em grumble. If we don't get out of here they'll wind up dead."

75

7

"Grumble" was hardly the word for it. Gaston told Captain Gringo he was insane, and Gaston was on his side. The others pissed and moaned about it taking forever to fill the big boilers with coconut water, a nutful at a time. But nobody had any better suggestions, and in the end most of the combined crew went ashore with Quico's corpse and the water drums. Gaston said he'd supervise, as he was bored with listening for radio waves and wanted to stretch his legs. Captain Gringo agreed. But he singled out the rebel called Angelo and told him he was counting on him to make sure everyone did his share. Angelo seemed surprised. But he smiled agreeably and said they could rely on him. It got the son of a bitch off the ship for the time being, anyway.

Captain Gringo led Porter and Gomez up into the conning tower as Gaston and Angelo supervised the new shore party. He put Gomez up in the crow's nest as lookout, knowing he could see out to the open sea over the island trees. He told Porter to get on the wireless set as he found a broom and started sweeping out the shot-up wheelhouse. Nobody else had seen fit to make the effort, and it was a pain in the ass to crunch around on broken glass.

Nothing could be done about the shot-out windscreens. There were steel shutters meant to be swung down in a fire fight. If they ran into heavy weather he knew he could steer, sort of, by squinting out through the peepholes.

He swept the glass out on the port wing and through a scupper into the water below. Ashore, he saw a skirted figure with copper glints to her hair walking with Angelo. He hadn't told Cathy to go or stay. Apparently she was the one Angelo considered his *mujer*. Leaving her to him might improve Angelo's disposition, particularly if they found some nice bushes, but it seemed a waste. Cathy was bright as well as pretty. Angelo was good-looking, but stupid. If she tied her future to his rebel kite it didn't figure to be a long one. Angelo didn't have the brains to be a guerrilla leader. He just had the arrogance. They'd already been picked up, once. The next time, Cathy would probably wind up dead.

The cook, one of the navy deserters, had gone ashore with the others. Captain Gringo made himself a sandwich, got a bottle of *cerveza* from the ice box, and headed for his cabin under the conning tower. The nice thing about running a gunboat with a skeleton crew was that there was plenty of room, at least. He'd taken the former captain's quarters as his own. Gaston and Porter had grabbed the mate's two cubbyholes.

He wondered if it might not be a good idea to ask Gaston and the other American to double up so that Angelo could have an officer's berth. It might calm Angelo down to have his heart's desire alone in a private cabin. He'd have to think about it. The idea of having Cathy getting humped by that Neanderthal, right next door, was sort of unpleasant to contemplate. But what the hell, Angelo had seen her first and he had enough to worry about without a mutiny over ass.

He fumbled his door open and ducked in to relax with his sandwich and suds. The only light, now that the generators were dead, came in through a narrow loophole in the armored porthole. But he could see the woman on his bunk well enough. It was Cielita. The little *mestiza* had taken off her clothes again, if she'd ever had them on since the last time they met down the companionway. He kicked the door shut with his heel and put the refreshments down on an end table before he said,

77

"You're going to get us both in trouble, Cielita. Don't you ever wear anything?"

Cielita said, "It is most hot. I mean the *air* in here. Can we not open the porthole? I tried, while I was waiting for you. But I can't seem to open it. So I have been suffering, getting hotter and hotter by the minute."

"I figured you might be hot," he grinned. She grinned back and said, "I think, back there when we were being shot at, we must have started something. I keep remembering how it felt to be naked in your so-strong arms. I keep remembering how nicely you kiss. When the others said they were going ashore, I thought how nice it would be to meet you again, in privacy."

"You don't beat around the bush, do you? Does anybody know you're here?"

"Of course not, I am a most discreet person. Would you have the others take me for a bad girl?"

"I guess not. How many of the others *have* taken you, up to now?"

Cielita looked hurt and said, "Don't say bad things about me, Deek. I may be a little naughty, but I am not wicked."

She saw he was just standing there, bemused. So she sat up, swung her knees between them, and leaned forward, still seated, to fumble at his pants, pleading. "Why are you teasing Cielita? Don't you think I am pretty?"

As she unbuttoned his fly, he ran a hand through her soft hair and said, "I think you're very pretty, but we'd better back up and think this thing through. Somebody's already jealous as hell and . . ."

"You like Catalina better, eh? I might have known. You think because she is whiter than me, she makes love better."

Then she hauled his confused limp shaft out and kissed it wetly.

He was still confused, but his shaft rose to the occasion with a mind of its own as Cielita began to inhale and exhale it, eagerly. He got to work on his other buttons as he realized what a swell way this was to assure Angelo he wasn't after Cathy. He knew Cielita would tell, and he knew that meant good-bye to any outside chance he might

said, cautiously, "I never sodomize a lady unless she asks me. Uh, did you say Angelo? The guy with the scar on his jaw?"

She wriggled her rump and said, "Yes. He thinks he is my lover. But I have grown most tired of him, lately. He has a most pathetic cock. Maybe that is for why he wishes to come in my back door."

He stopped what he was doing. Cielita moved back to take it all as she asked, "What is wrong? I like it this way. Do it faster."

He started moving, automatically, and it did feel nice, but his heart wasn't in it as he said, "Listen. If Angelo finds out about this, he's going to be mad as hell."

She said, "I know. He killed a boy in Gatun over me. Pound me harder. I am almost there."

So Captain Gringo politely made the lady come, and somehow in the process came himself. Cielita snuggled her head on his chest as they stretched out to recover. Sanity returned before his breath did. He said, "Listen, Cielita. We're going to have to keep this our own little secret. I don't want to fight Angelo."

"Pooh, I'm sure you'd win. I have knowledge of both your bodies and you are stronger than Angelo. You have a bigger cock, too."

"Oh, boy! You tell him *that* and somebody gets to die for sure! It's not important whether I can take Angelo or not. I want him alive. We've already lost one man. We can't afford to lose another. Can I count on you to keep this afternoon a secret?"

"Well, I might, if you promise for to be nice to me."

"Haven't I been nice enough, Cielita?"

"*Si,* just now. But what about later? If I am to be your secret *mujer,* you must *treat* me like your *mujer,* no?"

"I'll probably be on the bridge most of the night, Cielita."

"That is all right, *querido.* It may save having to explain some things to Angelo. He will know I am not on the bridge with you if I am in bed with him, no?"

"That sounds reasonable."

"Very well. I will take care of Angelo. But you must

take care of me. He leaves me most unsatisfied, but his lovemaking does tend to arouse me, eh?"

"I noticed."

She giggled and snuggled closer as she said, *"Mañana,* at this same time, I will come here to you and we will devour one another, eh?"

He didn't answer. Her little game sounded dangerous as hell as well as downright fatiguing. But on the other hand, if she got sore at him, she was in a position to cause a lot of trouble. So he patted her and said, "I'll be looking forward to it, *muchacha.*"

She giggled again and said, "It makes me so hot just to think of it. That snooty Catalina has no man at all and I will be taking turns with the two best-looking boys aboard."

"Jesus, you're not going to tell *Cathy,* are you?"

"I don't know. I haven't made up my mind. I will not tell silly Angelo. I might not tell silly Catalina. You see, she likes you. I am trying for to decide whether it would be more fun to keep her guessing or to tell her she does not have a chance with you."

He said, "Hell, let her suffer," and Cielita's laugh was downright dirty when she agreed. He knew she'd probably brag. But what the hell, Cathy wouldn't stick a knife in him. He hoped.

8

By sundown everyone was exhausted and complaining, and they hadn't gathered half the coconut water it would take to flush and refill the boilers. But then, ironically, the sky began to darken and it looked like rain for sure. So Captain Gringo called everybody aboard and told Angelo to form a detail and spread catch cloths on the deck. He wanted to send Angelo to bed too tired to ask questions. He was braced for an argument, but the scarfaced guerrilla simply nodded and said the idea made sense. When one of the others asked why they couldn't catch the scupper water off the rain-wet decks, Angelo surprised Captain Gringo by saying, "*Estupido,* the decks are salty and there is much loose paint as well as dust. Do you think we can run a steam engine with dirty salt water? We will spread tarps and run the fresh rainwater into fire buckets, the right way."

Captain Gringo went up to the conning tower, a little less sure of the situation. Angelo wasn't stupid. He just looked stupid. If he was nursing a grudge over Cielita, he was a hell of an actor, too. The *mestiza* had assured him Angelo suspected nothing. Neither one of them had made a play for Cathy. So what in hell was going on?

He told Gaston and Porter about the problem, leaving out the orgy, when he joined them in the radio shack. Gaston said, "It is *tres* simple. Some troublemaker is spreading false rumors. If Angelo is known as a possessive type, they are hoping to get the two of you into a fight by suggesting you are rivals. But since Angelo is the only

83

one sleeping with the little slut, what does it matter?"

Porter said, "I just picked up a wireless signal from a freighter over the horizon. They weren't talking about us. But they seem worried about a full gale off the coast. The freighter says they're meeting heavy weather and taking green water over the bows."

Gaston said, *"Merde,* one does not mention *gales* in these waters. Can't you smell the air around us?"

Porter sniffed and said, "Yeah, it smells like hot copper wires. I thought some of this radio shit was heating up. I don't know too much about Marconi's inventions."

Gaston said, "You do not smell hot electric wires. But we'd better make sure the acid-filled batteries are *tres* secure. What you smell is an approaching hurricane. We do not settle for gales on the Mosquito Coast. The hurricane was named by the local Indians for a most unpleasant god of the southeast sky. The Indians knew who they were talking about."

Gaston turned to Captain Gringo to add, "Dick, we have to get out to green water. If we are hit by a hurricane off a lee shore, we won't stand a chance."

Captain Gringo nodded but said, "We'll have to risk the first hour or so. They're draining the boilers already. The coconut water we have aboard won't do it. We need a few inches of rain before it'll be safe to light the oil jets."

Porter said, "I'm missing something. Are you guys serious about wanting to move out to *meet* the damned storm?"

Captain Gringo nodded and said, "We have to. Once the swells start sloshing around between these islands we'll be in the same position as a toy duck in a bathtub. The water can go from fifty feet deep to dry bottom every few minutes."

"Can't we run into the mainland and find a sheltered cove?"

"What mainland? It's mangrove swamp a good ten miles in from the apparent shoreline."

Gaston said, "The way the Great God Hurricane gets you in shoal water is to drop you on the bottom and burst every seam before he sends the next fifty-foot swell over you. Out at sea, one can ride over such waves.

Wind and water alone have a hard time popping rivets. Mix wind and water with sand and rocks and ooh, la! la!"

Captain Gringo walked out on the bridge wing. He saw Angelo's crew had spread canvas on the foredeck between the guns and bow. There wasn't a breath of wind stirring the palms ashore, now, in the purple light of the gloaming, but Angelo had been smart enough to weigh the canvas down with odds and ends of ship's gear. As a native, Angelo obviously didn't have to be told about the fickle weather down here.

They were at anchor on the lee shore of an island, but the oily-looking water moved up and down, slowly, and wavelets were starting to break on the beach. As he watched, the water level seemed to rise, quietly, until the nearest palm trunks were standing upright in smooth water. Then, just as slowly and quietly, dry land reappeared between them and the level dropped down and down until the beach seemed wider than they'd ever seen it before. He ducked back inside and said, "The ground swells ahead of the storm have arrived and there's not a sign of rain. We've got to get out of here."

Gaston asked, "How? We can't finish topping the tanks with raw sea water."

"We're going to have to. It means chancing a stalled engine with a fifty-fifty mixture of God-knows. But if we stay here we'll drown for *sure!*"

Gaston shrugged and said, "Very well, I shall attend to it. I'll signal when I'm ready to start the engines. You will of course wish to man the helm as we depart these delightful shores?"

"I haven't any place else to go. Get Angelo and his guys below. We may get to use that canvas yet, but tonight's not our night to flap around on deck."

Gaston left, muttering. Porter sighed and said, "I wish you guys could make up your minds. You seem to make up new plans every few minutes."

"Of course, I plan all the time. I just have to *change* them as I go because the world keeps pitching *curves!*"

Porter nodded and said, "I see. We'll worry about tomorrow once we make it through the night, right?"

"You sure are an optimist, Bill. Who told you to count on making it through the night?"

9

Captain Gringo manned the helm alone in the wheelhouse as *La Tortuga* fought for sea room, plowing through the foreswells of the storm. He'd sent the lookout below to keep him from catching pneumonia and because there was nothing to see up there in the darkness and horizontal rain. He'd sent Porter down closer to the center of gravity because the storm had filled the air waves with deafening static and because Porter said he was getting seasick. Gaston was in the engine room, trying to convince a nice Victorian steam engine that she certainly *could* run on the god-awful mixture in her boilers. They figured they were boiling about a third of the original wine laced brackish water, one-third coconut water, and one-third straight brine. Gaston said it all depended on how fouled the tubes were in the first place. Starting with clean tubes, they could hope to steam a full day or more on hard water. Since the previous crew had grossly mistreated the poor old tub, her engine could turn over through the night or stop any minute. They were running at full speed. Gaston had a theory that it was better to shoot the shit through the valves at high pressure and hope it all went through. So *La Tortuga's* heavy mass was making sixteen knots and didn't screw around with riding up and over the waves. Her stubby armored bow just smashed on through and took the green water as it came. Anyone on deck would have been washed overboard a while back. *La Tortuga* lay low in the water when the water was lying low. In heavy weather she thought she was half submarine.

He'd switched off the wheelhouse lights, since there wasn't anything inside he had to steer around, and he had to see out. He could just barely do that. He'd lowered the bullet-proof screens to keep the hurricane outside. The slit above the wheel was little more than a paler shade of blackness as he stared through it, squinting his eyes against the gusts and spray that kept coming in. From time to time a lightning flash informed him they weren't steaming into anything solid, but the momentary views of the wild churning sea was sort of stomach-wrenching. He mostly steered by compass, and if the little red binnacle light went out they were in trouble. Captain Gringo was no sailor, though he'd mucked about Long Island Sound in a cat-boat, as a kid. He trusted the compass to keep them headed away from shore and he trusted to his guts and balance to take the waves on port quarter, like a football player hitting the line with his left shoulder. *La Tortuga* seemed to ride the swells at that angle with less groaning and mysterious popping sounds from her innards. The seas were getting serious, now, with chains of ten- or twelve-foot breakers racing over long mountain ranges of ground swell. The wind had found a rivet-hole or something in the nearby darkness and kept moaning at him like an owl trying to lay a square egg. He stood at the wheel with his legs spread wide and he leaned back, clinging to the spokes, to keep himself in place and to have an easy view out the gun slit designed with a shorter man in mind. Aside from the worry about catching the wrong wave and flipping over, the chore would have been a bore.

He heard a hatch open behind him. He didn't turn his head in the darkness. The latch had given, or Gaston had come up to bitch about something. There was a brilliant flash of lightning and Captain Gringo swore as he saw the Great Wall of China bearing down on them in the form of churning foam. He ducked his head below the slit by bending his knees, still clinging to the wheel, and some son of a bitch shot a fire hose through the slit. Behind him, a woman's voice screamed in surprise and dismay. He was a little surprised himself. Cielita had said she wanted more, but he'd thought it was Angelo's turn and this was hardly the time or place.

The gunboat made it through the giant breaker and

the wind through the slit died as they rode through the trough below the storm. Catalina O'Hara picked herself off the wet slippery deck and staggered over to join him, saying, *"Madre de Dios,* I am soaked to the skin!"

"Welcome to the club, Cathy. What can I do for you? You can see it's more comfortable down below, and I'm not serving sandwiches."

Cathy groped for something to hang on to and he said, "Hey, don't get between me and the binnacle. I have to see the compass."

"I can't find anything else to hang on to," she protested.

La Tortuga shuddered as her bows began to feel another ground swell and he reached out in the dark for her, saying, "Here, get between me and the wheel."

He couldn't see in the dark, of course, so he'd grabbed her left tit instead of her shoulder. They both shifted his hand without comment as she moved into the space between his torso and the big mahogany wheel.

He put his hand back on the spokes, but his palm still tingled. She was soaking wet, all right, and her nipple had been hard as a rock. Cathy had her back to him, facing the same way. The back of her head didn't block his view enough to matter and her hair smelled like salt-water taffee. He said, "Hang on. We're on our way to the stars."

Cathy clung to the wheel with her own hands as she leaned back against him. He wore no underwear under his wet cotton, and though his hands were properly placed on the wheel with her, he could tell she had nothing on under the peasant blouse and wet skirt plastered to her flesh. The tropic night was warm as August in Ohio, but his own flesh was covered with goose bumps under the wet cloth. He wondered what she'd say if he took off his shirt.

The heavy iron bow rose slower than the swell and they shipped a wave that shattered on the forward gun turret and spat a bathtub full of foaming brine through the slit at them. He'd expected it and lowered his center of gravity to hang from the spokes with his butt just off the deck. Cathy caught it full in her face and fell back into his suspended lap. He laughed and held on as the shower subsided. He seemed to gain a certain strength in his grip as he became aware of the firm hemispheres of Cathy's buttocks in his open lap. As he hauled them back up, she was aware of his erection between her cheeks, through the wet cloth. She quickly straightened her legs and thrust her pelvis against the wheel hub, which only served to tighten her firm buttocks on the broomstick she'd been riding. She gasped, "Heavens, must you stand so close?" and he moved back. It felt as though he was withdrawing from her. It made him hot as a two-dollar pistol and must have had some effect on her. But she said, "I came up here hoping to find you alone."

He resisted the impulse to goose her with his shaft again as he said, "You found me. What's up? I mean, what *else* is up?"

She repressed a laugh and said, "I wanted to warn you. Some of the men in the band are plotting against you."

He said, "Oh, I knew that. What's *your* version?"

She pressed harder against the polished hub of the wheel, which came exactly up to her crotch as she stood with her legs straight. Since he had his legs spread wide to brace them, it lowered his own crotch to the same level, even though he was much taller than the girl. She said, "Somehow, I never would have guessed you had such short legs, Deek. Do you have to rub against me like that?"

"I'm not rubbing. The boat's rolling. You can leave if you're not comfortable."

She sighed and said, "I think we're both uncomfortable, but we must bear it for the moment. I overheard some of the guerrillas talking with some of the deserters. They seem ungrateful and most jealous."

"That's par for the course. I probably wouldn't get in so many fights down here if I was shorter and had black hair. The nickname, Captain Gringo, isn't always meant as a compliment. Most guerrillas think they're meant to be generals, and sailors who like to take orders don't desert. Did you overhear any plans, or are they just bitching?"

She said, "One of them mentioned Angelo. They said Angelo did not believe you had been hanging horns on him with Cielita. I found the idea grotesque, too. What on earth do you suppose they meant by that?"

An unexpected shift of the deck shoved his pelvis against her derriere and she gasped as the wheel hub slid between her thighs from front and his bound erection goosed her again from behind. He tried to keep his voice calm as he replied, "Oh, you know how it is. Guys are always trying to start a fight by telling some clown another man has been fooling with his girl."

Cathy said, "I know. Frankly, I don't think any man would have much trouble getting Cielita to misbehave. It's lucky for you it's me and not her up here alone with you right now, eh?"

"I don't know if you could call this luck. I'm starting to hurt. But let's stick to our plotters. Do you think they've sold their story to any of the others? How do *you* feel about it? Do you think I've been naughty with Cielita?"

She laughed and moved her rump against him mockingly as she replied, coyly, "As an educated guess, I would vow you had not been with any woman for some time, Deek."

He thrust boldly forward as he asked, "Oh? How educated a guesser are you, Cathy?"

She tried to slide off, found she couldn't, and stared out into the storm as she replied, "I won't try to tell you I'm a virgin, Deek. But this is getting silly. I think I'd better go."

"Don't you think you'd like to come? You're right about it being silly. It's gotten past silly and we're into cruelty to animals!"

Cathy laughed as she wriggled her derriere against him. He could tell she liked it and she probably felt safe. Nobody enjoyed cock-teasing like a woman who figured she was safe. She said, "You're just awful. I'll bet I'd be in trouble if you didn't have to keep your hands on this wheel, eh?"

They were in a quiet trough and the rudder wasn't fighting him at the moment. He took one hand off the spokes and reached down to open his fly. His liberated erection popped out with a relieved twang. So as long as he had his hand down there, he decided to haul her wet skirt up out of the way. Cathy, her own hands on the wheel for balance, gasped, "What are you doing?" and

90

he said, "Trying to get warm. Don't your legs feel better without that wet cotton clinging to them?"

"I am wearing no pantaloons!"

"Hey, it's dark and nobody can see."

She tightened her bare buttocks as he slid his shaft between them and protested, "You are not trying to see. You are trying for to feel!"

"Yeah. You said I was just awful and it feels great."

She giggled and relaxed a bit as the flesh between her cheeks and thighs began to arouse her. He guided the tip into place near a quivering opening and she said, "You are mad, and if you think that finger is playing with the right hole, you are stupid, too!"

He said, "You're dumber than that if you think it's my finger. Tilt your spine a little, huh?"

She said, "We can't do it standing up in a hurricane, you idiot!" But even as she protested she arched her spine. So he lowered his pelvis, took better aim, and thrust up into her as she gasped, "Oh, my God! You *can* do it standing up in a hurricane! What if somebody catches us?"

"Relax. Nobody's about to come up here and even if they did, it's pitch dark and you're only helping me steer, right?"

She started helping him indeed as he began to thrust in and out with his weight hanging from his hands on the spokes. She clung to the wheel, too, derriere out to welcome him home. She lowered her head between her arms and moaned, "Oh, this is very wicked. You *are* not to be trusted around poor women. I'll bet you *would* do this to Cielita if you got the chance!"

"Do you think I *have* done this to her, Cathy?"

"It is obvious you have been celibate for some time. This position would be most impossible with a man of more normal desires and dimensions!"

He said, "Yeah, it is sort of awkward. Let's turn you around and do it right."

He withdrew and suited deeds to action as she protested that she'd been about to climax. He got her tailbone braced on the hub of the wheel and took charge frontally as Cathy moaned, "Oh, no, it's too deep this way!" Then she wrapped her arms around him and kissed him wildly as she began to bump and grind. He clung to the wheel to keep them in position as he used his free hand to peel off as much of their wet clothing as he could without stopping. As he hauled her skirts up and off they had to stop kissing for the moment and she said, "This is the most naughty thing I ever heard of! Do you realize you were in me before we'd ever even kissed?"

He shoved it to her hard and said, "Yeah. How do you like it so far?"

"I love it, you beast! But I know I'll hate myself in the morning."

"Don't get ahead of yourself, Cathy. We might not be *alive* in the morning."

He'd almost forgotten where he was or what he was supposed to be doing when he felt the deck shift oddly under him and the rudder was starting to fight harder. It made the wheel spin harder from side to side and Cathy gasped, "Oh, Jesus, I'm coming again! Spin me upside down, *querido!*"

He said, "I'd love to, but I don't think it's a practical idea. Hang on. I'm coming, too, but we have to stop."

She asked him what he meant as he finished and somehow wound up on the floor atop her in the process. He didn't answer until he'd finished coming, knowing it might be the last he'd get for some time, if ever. Then he reached out to grab the wildly spinning wheel as he rolled off her, saying, "Get dressed. It's going to be crowded in here in a minute."

She sat up with a puzzled frown and asked, "What's wrong, Deek? The boat is rolling so strangely. I thought it was me, but . . ."

"The engines have stopped," he cut in, adding, "Hurry up. See if you can find my pants and help me slip them on."

As he experimented with the wheel, getting no response, Cathy put on her own clothes and got him into his pants, at least, before Gaston came in to shout, *"Merde alors!* I *told* you the valves would choke on all that salt! What do we do now?"

Captain Gringo said, "That's a good question. I'm open to any good suggestions. If we don't do something, and fast, *La Tortuga* will turn turtle in fact as well as name."

10

The sea anchor helped. Not a hell of a lot, but anything was better than taking a hurricane broadside. They lashed two beams into a huge cross, tied buckets and tarps to it for maximum drag, and let it out on a bow line. The water under their keel was maybe a mile deep. They wanted to keep it that way. So while the tangle they were tied to had nothing to hook into, it lay heavy and awash with most of its mass under water and out of the wind. *La Tortuga*'s superstructure caught the northeast wind like a big iron sail, of course. The results were that she lay dead in the water, but with her bows pointed into the wind and waves as the storm blew them any goddamned place it had a mind to.

It was all they could do. The only chance they had was the hope that they'd steamed further out to sea before the engines stopped than the storm could drift them before it blew over. So they just had to sit tight and sweat or pray, depending on their religious background, as *La Tortuga* headed for the Central American mainland, stern first.

After things quieted down a bit, he went back up in the conning tower. There was no point in trying to steer until Gaston, swearing a lot, did something about the stuck valves in the engine room. But Porter was curing his seasickness with a bottle of Jamaican rum and bed rest. There was an outside chance somebody, somewhere, knew the extent of the storm and where the hurricane's eye was heading. So after changing into dry white ducks, Captain Gringo got on the Marconi set.

The earphones were sticky and it was stuffy in the little room. He sat at the table under the dim Edison lamp and fiddled with the dials, only half aware how the damned thing worked. The world was changing too damned fast, these days. He was still a young man. But when he said he'd fought the last Apache, people looked at him as though he was Buffalo Bill. Nobody had said anything about fucking radio waves when he'd been learning his trade at West Point. The new telephone had the old military instructors confused enough. He owed his modest fame south of the Rio Grande to the fact that he was still one of the few men in any army who understood the new machine gun and the changed battle tactics new weapons called for.

He twisted the dial until he picked up distant dots and dashes. He found a pencil stub and started taking the message down on a pad. A Dutch three-islander, sending in English, was pissing and moaning about a shifted cargo and busted rudder, somewhere west of Aruba. They said the storm was subsiding, but they needed help. He was sorry as hell about that, but things were looking brighter for *La Tortuga* if the skies were clearing near Aruba. Hurricanes never turned south and Aruba was well to the northeast. That put them due south of the eye and meant they were catching the south swirl. Figuring the center moved twenty miles or so an hour, although the winds around the eye did more like a hundred, they should see a clearing before sunrise. The waves would be a bitch for at least another day or so. But once the wind stopped trying to shove them ashore, they could ride out any wave under clearing skies. He started to look for a map. Then he decided not to bother. He had no idea where they were. If they hit land they hit land. There wasn't a damned thing he could do about it even if he knew it was about to happen.

The signals from the Dutchman faded. They'd either changed wave lengths or sunk. It wasn't his problem. Wanted outlaws were relieved of certain social niceties. He knew nobody out there was about to give a damn if *he* had to send an S.O.S.

He'd already thought of that and dismissed the idea.

94

Drowning couldn't be much fun. Being shipwrecked in a mangrove jungle full of snakes and man-eating Indians sounded even grimmer. But except for Porter, who only faced prison, there wasn't a person aboard who wouldn't be shot or hanged by anyone kind enough to rescue them. They were in Colombian waters. Even a British or American vessel would be honor-bound to turn them over to Colombia. Although an American ship would probably return him to the States to hang, and of course any French vessel would take Gaston straight to Devil's Island. *His* first death warrant had been signed by Louis Napoleon!

The door opened as he searched for other signals. It was Cielita.

"I thought you were spending the night with Angelo."

"Pooh, no woman spends a night with Angelo. He goes to sleep as soon as he has made love once."

Cielita moved over, hooked her buttocks on the edge of the table, and opened her kimono to ask, "You like?"

He nodded, but said, "For Chrissake, I thought we agreed to play it cool! It will cause trouble if we're caught together, Cielita."

"Bah, who is going to catch us, eh? It is after midnight. Anyone who is not stuck at his post is asleep or seasick or both. Who is going to prowl about in such a storm?"

"Angelo, for openers. What if he wakes up to find you gone?"

"He won't. He had been drinking even before we went to bed. I think that is why he left me so unsatisfied. I want for you to satisfy me, Deek."

She slid closer and put an arm around his neck as she thrust a brown breast at his face, teasingly. He kissed it to be polite, but said, "I can't right now, honey. I want you, of course, but sailing backwards in a hurricane is sort of distracting. Can't you wait until *mañana* and *La Siesta?*"

She moved her other breast in position and said, "Kiss this poor thing. She is jealous of her sister." So he did. Her nipples were turgid and he could tell she wanted it bad. She began to stoke his hair as he nibbled and somehow, even though he knew better, his goddamned hand started roaming over her firm tawny flesh. It was cooler, now, and the electricity in the air was doing something funny to his hair as she ran her fingers through it. He stopped and said, "Listen, we'd better stop before it's too late, *querida*."

She leaned back provocatively, opening her thighs as she said, "It is already too late. What are you waiting for? Don't you want me?"

"Of course I do," he lied, "But not in public, for God's sake. This is a radio shack, not a stateroom with a lock on the door."

"Pooh, we can lock the door and turn out the lights. Nobody will catch us. That snooty white girl, Catalina, is sound asleep in her cabin and your other friends are busy."

"Oh, have you been talking to Catalina?"

"Just passing in the companionway. I think she thinks I am wicked. She knew I was going to join Angelo and the poor thing has no man of her own."

Cielita giggled and added, "If she knew how good you were she might wish for to steal you, no? But don't worry. I am keeping the secret of my *toro feroz* all to myself!"

He got up and locked the door as she watched, licking her lips. He switched off the light. He didn't want her even thinking about Cathy if he could help it, and the only way he could help it was by giving her what she wanted.

They both blinked in surprise as the light went out. He could still see her, weirdly. Cielita and everything else in the room was outlined in a ghostly green glow. It looked as though she'd been rubbed down with fireflies. She said, *"Nombre de Dios!* You look like a ghost!"

He held a hand out and stared down at the glowing hairs and nails. It looked spooky as hell. He said, "Saint Elmo's fire. All this electrical equipment around us has joined forces with the storm. I've never seen it indoors before, but the vessel's made of iron and we seem to be charged up some dumb way."

"Are we in danger, Deek? My flesh feels funny, like a kitten is licking me all over and, *ay muchacho,* I can see my very toenails!"

He said, "It's just some sort of electric thing. I've never heard of Saint Elmo's fire hurting anybody."

He started to take off his shirt. Cielita laughed and said, "You are so hot for me you are shooting sparks, no?"

Privately, he wasn't sure he could get it up. But she did look sort of interesting, jet black curves outlined in pale green fire.

He moved in, nude, to kiss her. Their lips struck tingling sparks as they made contact. She rose to press herself against him, letting her kimono spill to the floor in a shower of firefly flashes. He was wondering where the hell to lay her. There was only the bentwood chair and the table top. Cielita grasped his still limp shaft and said, "Oh, poor baby. He's afraid of the funny electricity, no?"

"I told you it was distracting."

Cielita laughed and slid to her knees, kissing him all the way down. He braced himself against the table as the vessel rocked and glanced down as Cielita started to kiss it up for him. It had only seemed *weird,* up to now. The sight of his glowing shaft being inhaled by a fiendish black and ghostly green face jolted hell out of him! The hairs on his belly were standing straight up, shooting tiny sparks. The part of his shaft in her wet mouth just felt great. The parts the air was hitting tingled like cold fire. She stopped, grinned up at him like a pretty demon, and said, "Oh, you are ready, aren't you?"

He said, "That's for damned sure!" as he helped her to her feet, put her rump on the table, and entered her with no further foreplay. Cielita leaned back against the bulkhead as he stood erect to put it to her. They could both see it moving in her pubic hairs as they stood wildly at attention like a burning bush. The metal edge of the table gave them both a mild electric shock each time his scrotum made contact. She said, "Oh, I have never felt anything like this! Have you?"

"No," he laughed. He'd started this as a chore, to keep the little slut contented. But he was now thrusting with feeling indeed. This would have been interesting as hell with anybody, and Cielita was pretty, in a cheap way.

97

Outlined in chalk marks of green fire she was downright glamorous.

She laughed and said, "Nobody is ever going to believe this happened."

He missed a stroke as that sank in. Then he started again and asked, "Oh? I thought we weren't going to tell anybody, *querida?*"

"I don't mean anybody aboard this old boat, Deek. But confess to me. Are you sure you will not, someday, wish for to tell someone about the time you made love to a woman who glowed in the dark?"

He said, "I don't think I will. You're right. Nobody would believe it."

She drew her knees up and hissed, "Oh, faster, my *toro!* I am almost there!" So he moved faster to please her. He was having a time getting there himself. It was up, but what the hell, he'd just had a great lay in the wheelhouse and as nice as this was, it was *work!* He wondered what Cathy would have looked like if she'd glowed like this against the wheel.

Cielita suddenly went limp and sighed, "Oh, *Madre de Dios,* that was wonderful. Don't you wish for to rest a moment, Deek?"

He said, "No," and kept moving. He couldn't come and it felt too good to stop. Common sense told him to fake an orgasm and rest. But he knew he'd have trouble getting it up again, once he stopped, and he knew Cielita would suspect something if he didn't take care of her. So he closed his eyes and pictured someone else. It was a trick he and probably a lot of other people had figured out to keep the fire going.

He started making love to all the women he'd ever wanted, especially the ones he'd never gotten. It was keeping him hard, but that was about the best he could manage. Cielita whimpered, "Enough, Deek! You are wearing me out!"

He said, "I thought you couldn't get enough, Cielita. It was your idea to start this, remember?"

"I know, but *por favor,* enough is enough! I have already come five times tonight."

"Oh? I only remember once."

"You did not answer, when I did just now. If you must know, I told Angelo he had not been satisfying me and tonight he did his duty. He is not as virile, but he kisses nice between the legs and . . ."

"You little slut," he growled, moving back to withdraw as he added, "You must be crazy. What made you take a chance like this if you'd already had all you wanted?"

She sniffed and said, "All right, if you must know, it was for to test you."

"Test me? What the hell were you testing. I screwed hell out of you just yesterday."

"I know. But somebody said Catalina had been up here alone with you and I thought you might have been bad with her."

He rolled her over, belly down and derriere up. He got the tip into position and thrust hard as he growled, "Does that feel like a tool that's seen a lot of use, doll?"

"Stop! You're putting it in the wrong way!"

He said, "I know. You wanted it. I'm giving it to you."

She began to sob and hammer the table with her clenched fists, shooting green sparks, as he sodomized her with more brutality than pleasure. He had to cure her of these sudden games and she'd said she didn't like it this way.

But apparently she did, once the shock wore off, for she started to move her tailbone teasingly, and the view of the fireworks display was exciting from this new angle. He suddenly knew he was going to make it over the hump and he started pounding. She gasped, "Gently, _querido!_ I have to get used to it in there and . . . Oh, _Madre de Dios_, what is happening?"

What was happening was that her clit was rubbing on the table edge and helping her out as he let himself go. He felt his legs turn to rubber as he finally came. Cielita pouted, "That was most wicked. Now both my holes feel most abused."

He said, "You know you liked it. Do you still think I've had it anywhere else tonight?"

"I can tell you have been true to me. But one of you

will have to go. I can't handle this much, now that Angelo is trying harder."

"Well, he saw you first, you know. I guess maybe the best thing would be for me to stand aside."

"But you are better, Dick."

"Make up your mind. You just said I was killing you. You know you can't talk like this to Angelo. He'd want to fight me and then you'd wind up with nobody. Gaston and Porter would kill Angelo if he won. Angelo's friends would kill me if I won. Be smart, honey."

She got up and weakly fumbled her kimono back on as she said, "I don't see why you men take this all so serious. I like you both."

"Well, we both like you. Would you share either of us with another woman?"

"No. I fear I have a most jealous heart."

There went a great idea. He shrugged and said, "It's settled, then. You'll just be Angelo's *mujer* for now and we'll say no more about it."

She moved over to kiss his forehead with a sigh before she said, "I know I must be hurting you. But you are right. You are taking it better than Angelo would. What is to become of you, now, with no woman of your own for to torture with your naughty thing, eh?"

"Oh, I'll manage, somehow."

"There is nobody else but that snooty Catalina on board. I don't advise you to try, with her."

"You figure she wouldn't play, eh?"

"If she did, you would regret it. She is spoken for."

"No shit? I thought you said she didn't have a man on board."

"Oh, she doesn't. That is why I was afraid you might have let her seduce you. But since she hasn't, I can tell you that none of the men aboard would touch her. She is the *mujer* of General Puma. A most dangerous man."

He blinked and asked, "General Puma? They had a general's girl friend locked up with Panamanian rebels?"

"Oh, General Puma is not in the Colombian Army. He is the leader of all the rebel guerrillas on the mainland. And Catalina is not his girl friend. She is his wife. They say he is very possessive about her."

100

11

When the sun finally rose, nobody could see it. *La Tortuga* was still afloat and the winds were dying, but the sky was still black with gangrenous glowing clouds. The engines were choked with salt and after dumping rain on them all night the fickle overcast ran dry as soon as it was wind-less enough to spread tarps on the deck. It probably wouldn't have worked in any case. *La Tortuga* wallowed each rain under in turn as she hung like a hooked carp on her sea anchor's line. The hurricane had wandered somewhere else for the moment, but the churned-up seas would take a while to settle down.

Captain Gringo held a private strategy meeting in the radio shack with Porter and Gaston, the only two men aboard he didn't suspect of plotting against him. He let Gaston have the floor until the sardonic little Frenchman had spilled all the bile he felt toward triple-titted engineers who couldn't design engines for sea-going ships that ran on sea water. They all agreed there was little point in working on the engines until they could rinse them out with fresh water. Porter suggested that since they seemed to be headed, backwards, toward the mainland, fresh water should be no problem in a while.

Gaston snorted and said, "*Mais non.* We shall no doubt wind up in a fresh-water swamp, upside down. The waves will be rolling in through the mangroves at least a mile."

Captain Gringo said, "Let's stick to getting ashore in

a more or less upright condition. If we can hook the bottom with our regular mud hooks we ought to be able to keep our stern out of the jungle. When the surf abates we can take the launch in and explore for a fresh-water creek."

Gaston said, "But of course. No doubt no government patrols are prowling about, and of course the Indians will welcome us with open arms."

Captain Gringo said, "I've been thinking about those Indians. Do you remember how we made friends with Blanca's band, that time?"

Gaston said, "A fluke. That albino sorceress saw your cock before she could put a poison arrow in you. I was talking to Gomez about her. He said the temporary alliance you forged between the San Blas and the Panamanian rebels didn't last. In any case, we are nowhere near the San Blas country. Any Indians we meet will be *tres* savage. Attempts by the local Hispanics to either exterminate them or make them go to church in pants has a way of making anyone a bit truculent, *non?*"

Porter said, "What the hell, we've got all sorts of guns and a big gang on our side."

The two soldiers of fortune looked at him with mutual pity and he asked, "Okay, what did I say that seems so stupid?"

Captain Gringo said, "The first rule in any rebel band is that guys who rebel in the first place tend to rebel in the second. We've got at least one, maybe two cliques of troublemakers aboard. So watch your back."

Gaston nodded and added, "At the moment we are all, literally, in the same boat. Nobody has tried to take this vessel away from us, because nobody knows how to run it. The moment we are on terra firma, there the old rules apply."

Porter asked, "Why don't we just ditch 'em and take off on our own?"

Gaston said, "*Merde alors!* One does not ditch anyone in the middle of an ocean! Where do you suggest we trot off to, and do you intend to walk or ride?"

Captain Gringo said, "It's not that simple in any case. Most of the guys are simple jerk-offs who'll wind up dead

102

if we leave them on their own. We owe it to them to leave them somewhere reasonably safe, and the Mosquito Coast ain't it."

Gaston sighed and explained, "He has these most distressing views on the loyalties of command. They obviously mixed him up at West Point."

Porter nodded and said, "I *heard* they taught weird subjects there. Just what do you think they're planning to pull on us, Dick?"

Captain Gringo shrugged and said, "The usual shit. Everybody wants to be a chief. Nobody wants to be an Indian. Some cocksucker's been trying to get me into a fight with Angelo. I think I've got that under control. There seems to be one troublemaker stirring up the navy deserters and another one spreading shit among the rebels. For all I know it's the same he or she."

Gaston cocked an eyebrow and asked, "Do you suspect one of the girls?"

"I don't know. I don't think Cielita has enough brains to plot her way to the cookie jar. Does the name, General Puma, mean anything to you?"

Gaston nodded and said, *"Oui,* I have heard about him in the *cantinas.* He is a good man to stay away from in our business. He is said to be a dedicated Panamanian Nationalist and a hell of a fighter. Unfortunately he does not get on well with soldiers of fortune. He hates all foreigners as much as he hates Colombia. He seems to suspect that any outside help Panama might get will result in outside interests trying to control his country. But why do you ask? His headquarters are said to be somewhere along the trail between Chagres and Panama City. I don't think he controls any guerrilla bands this far down the coast."

"I hope not. It seems our Cathy is General Puma's wife."

"Did she tell you this?"

"No. I just got it on the grapevine. I guess she doesn't want it spread around too much. But it explains why they let a woman speak for them. I don't know about the sailors, but if Cathy hollered 'froggy' hard enough, the rebel half of our crew might jump."

Porter asked, "So what? You're on good terms with Cathy, aren't you?"

Gaston put a finger to his nose and said, "Ah, that is the problem. I just told you her powerful and dangerous husband does not like our breed. If he were to even suspect his wife and Dick were, ah, good friends . . . But it could be worse. At least *we* know you haven't been in her pantaloons, eh, my old and rare?"

Captain Gringo didn't answer. Gaston sniffed again and sighed, "Oh, you stupid son of the bitch! My nose is never wrong! Haven't I told you over and over again to be careful about married Hispanic women?"

Captain Gringo answered, "Look who's talking. We didn't do it in here. So stop sniffing around. I'm not worried about what General Puma thinks of me. He'd think it, anyway, once our secret troublemaker had a word with him. I can think of a dozen reasons for Cathy not leveling with us. I don't think she's behind the gossip. It wouldn't be aimed at her if she was. We've got to find out who it is, though, and fast. We have the Indian sign on everyone, out here on the water where they're aware we're useful. If we intend to keep control on shore, the troublemaker has to be caught before anything ugly happens."

He turned to Porter and said, "Bill, you'd better get on the wireless and make sure no Colombian gunboat is headed our way in the wake of the storm. I'm going up in the crow's nest to see if we're anywhere near shore. What shape is our rear turret in, Gaston?"

Gaston shrugged and said, "It failed to blow overboard last night. I have no idea if the guns fire or not. Why do you ask?"

"Hell, we're drifting in stern first."

"You expect to shell some mangrove trees?"

"We might have to, if they're occupied. We can't move until we get fresh water for the boilers. So anyplace we land has to be ours until we're through with it."

Leaving Porter in the radio shack, he went out and started up the ladder to the masthead. But Gaston stopped him and asked, quietly, "Wait. I know this is none of my business, Dick, but it is still my business if I am to make plans for the future."

"What are you talking about, damn it?"

"The amorous nature of my associates, of course. If you did not lay Cathy in there, you most definitely laid someone else, and there is only one other woman aboard."

"So?"

"*Merde alors!* Did not Gomez tell you Cielita belongs to Angelo and is not Angelo one of the rebel leaders?"

"Hey, don't worry, we got it straightened out."

"Oh, my poor trusting child, don't you know *any- thing* about women? We men only brag about our con- quests. Women *gloat!*"

12

The general circulation of the Caribbean is clockwise. The counter currents near the shores run counterclockwise. It was anybody's guess where they were as they drifted between two offshore keys and wallowed on, stern first, toward the low dark shoreline of what could have been the mainland or a bigger island among the Mulatas. Captain Gringo was about to order the mud hooks to be dropped when Porter came out of the radio shack and said, "I just picked up a message in English. It seems the Colombian government has declared us pirates. They've put out a description of this gunboat and they've posted a bounty on us, dead or alive."

Captain Gringo nodded and said, "I figured they might. It's hardly fresh news that they're annoyed with us."

"Wait. There's more. I told you they were sending in English. It seems a British cruiser is steaming down the coast at flank speed, with eight-inch guns they've been dying to try out. They just asked Colombia if they minded terribly if they used for us some target practice. Colombia said to go right ahead. They said they'll swap a gunboat for the elimination of such dangerous pirates any day."

Captain Gringo stared at the tree line ashore and said, "I don't think it'll hurt to drop anchor a little closer in, after all. With luck, the cruiser won't want to risk uncharted shallows and what the hell, if we're already touching bottom they won't be able to sink us."

"Do you think we have a chance of fighting them off, Dick?"

"Have you been drinking again? Even if we had a full-trained gun crew, which we don't, and all our shells were reliable, which they're not, you don't take on eight-inchers with four-inchers."

"They blow bigger holes, huh?"

"More important, they blow them at longer range. If that Limehouse cruiser spots us it won't move in close enough for us to reach her with our pop guns. She'll sit well out of our range and lob eight-inchers at us like she's pitching horseshoes. You may have noticed we don't get to dodge until the engines are running again."

Porter looked as though he was about to throw up. Captain Gringo smiled and said, "Relax, we'll be against the shoreline in a few minutes and what the hell, we're painted gray."

"Dick, those goddamned trees are green."

"Good thinking. Get on the wireless set and let me know if they spot us."

"Do you expect them to *tell* us, for Chrissake?"

"No. I expect them to send 'Tallyho' in Morse. If they thought we were listening in, they wouldn't be sending in the clear. This radio idea is still new. By the time everybody starts using them the Royal Navy will have to think up some codes. Fortunately, they don't think we're worth the trouble. So get back on the air and *listen,* for God's sake!"

Getting rid of Porter, he went to the foot of the mast and shouted up for the lookout's attention. When the sailor looked down, Captain Gringo yelled, "Watch for smoke over to the northwest and don't waste time coming down when you do. Fire your pistol."

Not waiting for an answer, he ran aft to the engine room hatch and slid down the ladder. Gaston and a couple of the deserters had the cylinder heads off and were banging on the pipes with wrenches. He yelled above the noise, "Leave that for now, Gaston. I want you topside. We may have company dropping in on us any minute."

Gaston followed him up to the afterdeck and he explained the situation. Gaston stared shoreward and spat before he said, "Porter is most unfortunately right. This gray paint is meant to make us hard to see at sea. That jungle wall is spinach green. Even if we run aground just offshore, we should stand out like the most sore thumb."

"I know. I don't suppose **there**'d be any green paint in the ship's stores?"

"*Merde,* what would green paint be doing aboard a gray gunboat?"

"Turning it into a green gunboat, if there was any aboard. I don't suppose we have a thousand cans of spinach in the galley either, huh?"

Gaston laughed, despite his worries. He said, "I don't remember *one* can of spinach. I like your idea, but to camouflage this vessel, one would need camouflage paint, *non?* The only paint in the stores is this same horizon gray. There may be some cans of white, for the trim. But I doubt the cruiser would take us for an iceberg this far south."

Captain Gringo said, "Copper. We've got all sorts of copper or brass fittings on this tub. They'll have extra demijohns of battery acid, too!"

Gaston started to ask him what on earth he meant. Then the little Frenchman nodded and said, *"Oui,* copper dissolved in acid equals green. But there is not enough time, and, even if there was, you can't use copper acetate for paint. It would corrode everything you splashed it on, including the splashers!"

"Stop being such a pessimist. Help me get a detail together and started. We'll mix a thick green goo and neutralize it with baking or washing soda. I know there's some lye in the galley. We'll thin it out with the regular gray paint and maybe throw some shoe black or something in it. The idea is for each bucket of paint to wind up a different disgusting shade of dirty green. We don't have to do a neat job. We can let some of the original gray show, as long as we streak it up with lots of green."

"I think I'm going to vomit. Aside from sounding *tres* fatiguing, your idea is **disg**usting a man who once studied art."

"How do you feel about standing off a cruiser with these antique four-inch guns, Gaston?"

"Merde alors, I would rather help you paint this damned thing pink!"

13

H.M.S. Dunraven was not, in truth, steaming at flank speed as she cruised along the Mulata chain. Her skipper didn't trust the charts and her skipper was a very good officer who'd worked too hard for his gold braid to lose it on a perishing dago reef. He'd ordered dead slow and had a leadsman on the bow as they followed the channel between the offshore keys and the mainland, guns trained on the jungle-covered shore. The skipper was out on the starboard wing, where he had a clear view fore and aft as well as toward the mucking jungle. A junior officer stood at his side, binoculars trained on the trees. The skipper did not allow small talk on the bridge, so there wasn't any as each man did his duty for Queen and Country.

H.M.S. Dunraven rolled sedately as she crawled. The seas were subsiding and the sun was out again at last. The junior officer knew it was going to be hot as hell by noon, and he wished he wasn't wearing a choke collar. But he knew better than to suggest less formal kit. The skipper allowed them to wear white in the tropics, period. There was no need to muck about in open collars just because the perishing natives couldn't stand a little heat.

The uncomfortable officer stiffened, adjusted the focus of his glasses and murmured, "I say, sir. There seems to be a vessel up that inlet."

The skipper said, "I was beginning to wonder about your eyes, Forsythe. I make her out a coastal schooner, with my *naked* eyes. She must have taken shelter from the ruddy storm that tidal creek.

"Shall I take the longboat in to investigate her, sir?"

"Whatever for? We're looking for a gunboat, Forsythe. Does that bloody sailboat look like a gunboat to you?"

"Nossir, but she is a strange vessel and I thought. . ."

"You *thought,* Ensign Forsythe? Great balls of Jesus! When did the Royal Navy order you to think, young sir?"

"Sorry, sir. No excuse, of course."

Mollified, the skipper said, "We're guests in these waters, Forsythe. Can't muck about with every native craft we encounter. The blighters probably don't speak English. It's probably a fishing schooner."

"This far down the coast, sir?"

"Why not? It's their coast, isn't it? She may have been blown here by the hurricane. She may be a bloody pearl poacher or a smuggler. It's not our concern. R.N. has agreed to help the Colombians out with that pirate crew who stole a gunboat. We never offered to police their perishing coast for them. Forget the schooner. We're looking for a bloody gunboat."

The junior officer raised his glasses with a silent sullen curse. Another officer came out on the wing to say, "The channel seems to be shoaling, sir. Permission to swing seaward?"

The skipper thought and said, "Permission denied. We're safe enough at this speed and I fancy the range. We're cruising just far enough out to be safe from that pirate gunboat's four-inchers. Any further and we couldn't see the bloody shore enough to matter."

The mate went back inside. The skipper stood facing into the faint breeze, hands behind his back, a smug expression on his face. All was right with the world. They were moving between a point and an offshore key, but he could tell by the quiet chop ahead that the water was deep enough for his keel if they stayed mid-channel.

A few minutes later, Forsythe muttered, "I say, that's a bit rum."

The skipper glanced abeam, saw nothing, and asked, "What do you see, damn it?"

The junior officer adjusted his focus again and said, "I'm not sure, sir. For a moment I was sure I was looking at another ship over there. Then the light shifted."

He raised the glasses again and said, "By Jove, there *could* be something over there, against the trees."

The skipper frowned and asked, "What do you mean, there *could* be? Do you see anything or not? Hand me the glasses!"

Forsythe did so, and precious seconds were lost as the older man adjusted the focus to his own vision. He aimed them at the shoreline and muttered, "Where, damn it? I see nothing but a lot of ruddy salad greens."

"Just to the west of that palm, sir. It's an odd sort of outline."

The older man swept the glasses back and forth, then locked on the strange pattern against the jungle wall. He said, "I see it. Bit weird, eh what? Looks like a bloody form of some kind, made of bloody glass. Trick of the light. It does look rather shippish, but we're seeing faces in the wallpaper."

"Faces in the wallpaper, sir? I'm afraid I don't understand."

"You never spent much time in a gloomy bedroom with floral wallpaper as a lad, then. It's a very common quirk of the human eye. I remember an absolutely ghastly old witch that used to peer out of my aunt's wallpaper at me. I seriously doubt the artist who designed the paper planned it, but the eye sees what it's looking for in random designs and small boys are more worried about witches than begonias, what?"

"Are you saying that vessel over there is an optical illusion, sir?"

"I hardly think anyone built a gunboat out of bushes, dear boy. I said I could see the ruddy outline. I agree it looks very much like a low-slung vessel with a conning tower between perishing gun turrets, but have you ever seen green guns? It's obviously just a random pattern in the jungle growth. We're all keyed to see a gunboat, ergo, we've started seeing gunboats. Unfortunately, that one seems to have tree trunks and vines showing through it."

Forsythe was too polite to demand the binoculars back and the damned target, whatever it was, was moving astern as they steamed on. He cleared his throat and asked, "Couldn't we just lob a shell into it to make sure, sir?"

The skipper lowered his glasses and shot his subordinate a thunderstruck look as he sputtered, "Lob a what, goddamn it? Have you any idea what an eight-inch shell costs, Forsythe? We don't *lob* shells in Her Majesty's Navy. We fire them into enemy craft or we keep them in the perishing magazines!"

"I'm sorry, sir. I know I'm overstepping my bounds, but I'm certain that was a real vessel of some kind. They may have disguised it with branches and vines, but. . ."

"That will just about be enough, Ensign Forsythe! In the first place it is not a vessel of some kind, and in the second, even if it was, we do not, repeat *not* fire on vessels of *some kind*. We fire at identified enemy targets and that, sir, is not an identified enemy target. It's a perishing pile of driftwood and greenery against the perishing shore."

"If you say so, sir."

"I do say so. I'm not a total idiot, whatever you young pups say to the contrary in the wardroom. I said I saw your bloody phantom. I know it's possible to paint even an elephant gray and green. But before you question an old man's eyesight, forget that pattern in the jungle growth and reconsider the *water*."

"Water, sir?"

"Water. Wet stuff. The funny stuff we float on. How deep would you say the draft is, over there against those bloody trees?"

Forsythe's neck reddened as the skippers words sank in. He sighed and said, "You're right, sir. Those mangroves can't be standing in more than half a fathom."

"Quite. And *La Tortuga* draws at least nine feet, according to her former owners. Do you still want to fire on that brush pile, or would you rather put a torpedo into her?"

Forsythe didn't answer. He knew the old man was going to haze him about his phantom gunboat at mess, and doubtless for the next few days.

112

But the skipper wasn't as unreasonable as his underlings considered him. He was an old pro, with a job to do and an assigned sector to cover. So, having put the eager ensign in his place, he said, "We'll finish this sweep to the end of the Mulatas. Then, if we haven't spotted the pirates the easy way, we'll poke into every ruddy cove on the return sweep. Remember where you saw your Flying Dutchman and I'll let you have a closer look when we pass this way again. What kind of a launch party did you have in mind, Forsythe?"

The ensign hesitated, not sure his leg wasn't being pulled. He said, "Oh, I thought I'd just nip over in a gig and see what it looks like close up, sir."

The skipper shook his head and said, "You'll do no such thing. If you go in at all, you'll take a detachment of marines and a machine gun. I still say we were seeing faces in the wallpaper, but there's no sense taking chances. If there's nothing there, the exercise won't hurt anybody. If by any chance that *was* a real whatever back there, I want you to be able to deal with it properly."

Ensign Forsythe nodded, pleased. The old man stared ahead as the narrows approached. It was too late to admit it, but that wonky clump of greenery *had* looked rather like a Clyde-built gunboat and he was dashed if he could figure out any way that nature could have copied those lines with random growth. Whatever it was was still within range of his stern guns. It was rather tempting to fire a salvo into it and see what happened.

But he'd already stated an opinion and British officers never changed a stated opinion without a damned good reason. If he wasted Her Majesty's ammunition on blowing up a mess of soggy brushwood he'd never live it down. They'd find out what it was for sure on the return sweep.

And so *H.M.S. Dunraven* steamed sedately on while aboard the gunboat W. S. Porter turned to Captain Gringo and sighed, "Jesus, I thought we were gonners for sure. They came too soon for us to finish our green zebra stripes, but your idea sure worked."

Captain Gringo saw Gaston coming out of the turret and frowned down from the seaward wing as the dapper

113

little Frenchman gingerly made his way over the sticky wet paint and came up the ladder grinning.

The tall American greeted him with, "You crazy bastard. You were swinging those fucking gun barrels like saloon doors on pay day!"

Gaston joined them and said, "But of course. I had my sights trained on that cruiser as it passed."

"I noticed. They must be blind as bats or they'd have noticed, too! Next time, hold *still* when I tell you to! Did you really think you could stop a cruiser with a lousy four-inch shell?"

"Mais non, but one must offer such resistance as one is able. Frankly, I was sure they'd spot us. You made a distressing mess of our port side with that ungodly *verdigris* slop, but we are a pistol-shot out from the mangroves, the mangroves are a different shade of green, and we are still one-third gray."

Captain Gringo shrugged and said, "I guess that's what did it. We broke our outline up and, besides, they were expecting to see a solid gray gunboat."

He swung his gaze to the distant smoke plume of the cruiser and added, "Okay, that's that. We'll take the launch and explore the shore for fresh water. If we fill the boilers and condenser tubes and let them soak overnight, they ought to flush fairly salt-free when we drain them and fill up again. What do you think about just a little heat to speed things up without evaporating any more salt on the metal?"

Gaston shrugged and said, "You have this odd habit of getting way ahead of yourself, Dick. Were you not listening when I observed that we were hard aground?"

Captain Gringo stared down at the muddy water all around them and said, "Okay, we drifted into shoal water and the tide seems to have dropped us in the mud for now."

"Dick, I took a sounding as soon as we stopped moving. We draw nine feet. The water here is less than five feet deep.

"So we're sort of *stuck* in the mud. First things first. We get the power back. Then we run a kedge line out to deep water and haul ourselves out of the goop with our anchor winch. We're not going anywhere until we get the engines working, in any case. Let's get some water drums and the machine gun in the launch. We'll leave Porter, here, in command."

Porter looked stricken and asked, "Are you serious?"

Captain Gringo nodded and said, "Sure I'm serious, Bill. What's the problem? You don't have to worry about moving the vessel or manning the gun turrets while we're gone. You just have to stand around looking important."

Porter asked, "Why not put Angelo, Gomez, or one of the other semi-leaders in charge?"

"Because we want to keep them semi-leaders. We know there's some resentment aboard. Even if there wasn't, these rebel types are funny about giving anything you give them back. If I made one of those exsailors or guerrillas a temporary skipper, he might opt for a permanent job, and we've got enough to worry about. I'm leaving you in command because I want it that way if and when we get back."

"But, Jesus, I'm no professional soldier, Dick! What the hell would I be able to do if they turned on me?"

Captain Gringo shrugged and said, "The same thing I would. Die, if they caught me napping. But what the hell, you're a big guy, and blue eyes seem to make people down here think you're a born killer. Just act like you know what you're doing and nobody else will tumble to the fact that you don't. You see, *they* don't know what they're doing, either. Very few people ever do."

He saw Porter was frightened, so he slugged him on the arm and added, "Hey, don't worry. The one or more factions plotting against us are planning to nail me first. They'll be too surprised by the switch to turn on you before they've had time to make up a whole new scheme. By the time they argue out who's going to do what with what and to whom, we should be back, and the game starts all over again."

"I hope you're right. What if you don't get back?"

"Beats the shit out of me. If I'm dead, it won't be my problem."

14

"Shoreline" was a poor description of where the map said the sea ended and the land began. Neither the shifting silt nor the soggy vegetation of the Mosquito Coast had ever read a map. The so-called coast was a vast morass of mangrove swamp, salt marsh, palmetto hummock, and twisted tidal creek between lagoons both great and small.

They left Gomez aboard with Porter. Gomez spoke enough English to match up with Porter's lousy Spanish and if they couldn't trust Gomez they couldn't trust anyone aboard *La Tortuga.*

They assigned two men to each of the four sweeps propelling the whaleboat-sized launch. They weren't really in that much of a hurry, but the extra crewmen would come in handy if and when they found fresh water. The water drums took up more room than everyone aboard. Gaston manned the tiller in the stern. Captain Gringo rode in the bow with the machine gun trained ahead. They knew any fresh water they found would be running down from the higher ground inland, so they tried to work their way deeper into the mess as they explored it. This wasn't easy. The channels hairpinned all over the place and tended to choke up with trees as the waters shoaled toward dry land. An hour from *La Tortuga,* Captain Gingo ordered them to land on a hammock. He leaped ashore, if you wanted to call something that felt like a big wet sponge a shore, and hauled the bow into place with the painter, leaving the machine gun where it was. Gaston crawled over the water casks to him to ask, "What do you expect to find here, Dick? The water all around is pure brine." Captain Gringo said, "I know. I'm going to shinny up a palm. If we can spot some cypress near enough to matter . . ."

"Mais oui. Cypress only grows where its roots can stand in fresh water. But let me scale the heights. This is a task for a monkey, not a moose. I can climb higher without breaking the poor tree, *non?"*

Captain Gringo nodded and Gaston started up the rough palmetto trunk. The eight men in the launch hadn't come ashore and were muttering among themselves about something. Captain Gringo wondered if he should have brought the machine gun ashore.

He'd expected Gaston to yell down yes or no. But his companion slid down quietly to say, "No cypress. Ship. I make it a schooner, about a mile or less, over that way. It must be anchored in a deep water cove."

Captain Gringo thought before he said, "Deep water means *running* water. She must be in a river mouth. River water is fresh."

Gaston shook his head and said, "Forget the damned river. I just told you someone has possession of the same. We'd better head the other way, *non?"*

Captain Gringo went over to the boat and said, "All right, *muchachos,* this is the way it is. There's a schooner anchored up ahead in a river estuary. She may be friendly. She may not. Her people could be harmless fisherman who sheltered here from the storm. They could be those clowns who shot us up the other day. The river water will be fresh and we need fresh water. What do you say?"

The boat crew muttered among themselves. One of the men said, "There must be other freshwater streams in this swamp, no?" But another snorted, "Who cares? I am tired of rowing. I say we ask for water most politely and kill the bastards if they won't behave like good neighbors!"

There was a mixed review to this suggestion, mostly in favor of it. So Captain Gringo nodded and said, *"Viva la Revolucion.* Let's sneak in and look them over before we ask to use their tap."

Meanwhile, a little over an hour's steam beyond the

crippled *La Tortuga, H.M.S. Dunraven* lay dead in the water as the skipper watched his captain's gig returning from the god-awful mess off his bows.

The charts showed a passage between that island to his port and the mainland to starboard. But the hurricane winds had dealt harshly with the low island and it was little more than a sand bank, swept bare of its trees. The perishing trees all seemed to be floating in the bloody channel ahead, and some of them were jolly big blighters. *H.M.S. Dunraven's* armored bows could reduce anything they hit to kindling, but he had his screws to think about and, more important, *floating* timber should be bobbing in the slight swell. The raft of debris ahead didn't move as the water swished back and forth through the tangle.

Ensign Forsythe came up the ladder and joined the skipper on the bridge wing to report, "You were right, sir. The channel ahead is shoal. Last night's storm shifted a lot of sand along with the roots of what used to be an offshore jungle. We'll have to move out to sea and go around."

The skipper frowned. When he'd been a junior officer he'd known better than to tell his skipper what he had to do. The abolition of flogging in the R.N. had certainly made hash of basic discipline.

He tried to ignore the heat and his own annoyance as he said, "I'll be the judge of what I have to do, young sir. We can't patrol for pirates cruising out beyond the Mulatas."

"But, sir, the passage ahead is treacherous."

" 'Pon my word, you ruddy pipsqueak. I haven't finished speaking! Don't you *want* to be promoted, someday, Ensign Forsythe?"

"I stand corrected, sir. My apologies for speaking out of turn."

"Accepted. As I was about to say, I can't risk Her Majesty's hull plates in new uncharted waters. We've covered two-thirds of the ruddy Mulata chain and the storm probably put the bloody pirates on the bottom in any case."

"Are we turning back, then, sir?"

"The R.N. never turns back. We are making another

sweep in the reverse direction. This time we'll move even slower and have a good hard look at every inch and inlet. Then, if we haven't spotted anything, we can break off the patrol with a clear conscience."

Forsythe looked relieved and asked, "Have I permission to investigate that wonky whatever I spotted up the coast, sir? I marked the position on the chart."

"Oh, very well. I still say it's a pile of floating brush, but we're in no great hurry. We've time for a spot of tea before we have to turn this bleeding mass of machinery around. Have you had your quinine this morning?"

"Yessir. Dissolved in gin, of course."

"Only way to get it down. You'd better have another and issue the same to your shore party. Lord knows what sort of bugs you'll meet when you row shoreward to investigate your mirage."

15

The river estuary's flood waters had built sandy banks and the open water was a quarter mile across. The schooner lay at anchor in midstream. She was a modern vessel with a sixty-foot steel hull, painted park-bench green. Her masts and trim were palm-trunk gray. She wouldn't look camouflaged to the casual eye in port, but she'd not been painted like that to stand out against a jungle shoreline.

As Captain Gringo and Gaston peered out through the reeds of the sand bank they'd landed on, Gaston said, "That's the species of pig we met before. Regard the weaponry on her stern."

Captain Gringo squinted at the two men manning a brass-bound Gatling mounted on the cockpit rail and said, "Tell me something I didn't know. What the hell are they pointing that gun at? What are those little critters in the water?"

They both watched as a small black object swam toward the stern of the mysterious schooner. Then a brown arm reached up and handed something to a third man aboard the vessel. Gaston nodded and said, "Pearl divers. They're pearl poachers, operating without a license from the government. One can see, now, why they fired on what they thought was a government gunboat."

"Yeah, nobody likes to pay taxes. But why are they covering their own divers with that Gatling gun? It makes no sense."

Gaston said, "Yes, it does. The men in the water are

Indians. Probably Caribs or those poor creatures the locals call *los perleros,* a mixed breed of refugees and runaways who manage to survive along these coast like your Cajuns near the Mississippi. It is my guess the crew of that pearl poacher has been recruiting help at the point of a gun."

One of the men from the boat behind them crawled through the reeds to join them. He asked what was up and Captain Gringo said, "They're outlaws. They've enslaved some local fisherfolk. Go back and fetch me the machine gun."

The sailor nodded and eased back. Gaston asked. "Are you mad, Dick?"

"What's eating you now? They're in machine gun range. I'll just dust that Gatling gun off and sweep the deck with plunging fire and . . ."

"Merde alors, they are diving for pearls right off the stern!"

"So what? I'm not going to aim at the Indians in the water."

"Pearl oysters do not live in *fresh* water, you idiot. Ergo, that estuary is *salt* water! Ergo, this is not our fight. Don't we have enough enemies looking for us?"

Before Captain Gringo could reply the Gatling gun aboard the schooner opened up with a brassy chatter and they both flinched. The gun crew was tap-dancing slugs off the water at a small bobbing dot and Gaston sighed, "Idiot, *dive!* The poor bastard is trying to get away, but he's not going to make it. *Perleros* are fine swimmers, but they know nothing about gunfire!"

Captain Gringo's breath caught in his throat as the line of gunfire splashes blocked his view of the swimming Indian. The gun crew stopped firing and the water rolled smoothly where the fugitive's head had been. It looked as though they'd gotten him.

Then Gaston swore, *"Merde!* Not so *soon!"* as the head popped up again, making their way at right angles to the stern of the schooner. The pearl diver was confused and headed into deeper water. He must have thought speed was more important than concealment and he really swam nicely on the surface. But the surface was a dumb place to be. Both white men gasped, "Jesus, dive!" as the Gatling opened up again. The pearl diver tried to swim faster. But nobody swims faster than a bullet. The stream of lead swept over the bobbing head. The white splashes were tinged with red as the Indian rolled over, went under, and then floated belly up as the gun ceased fire. The current was seaward and the corpse was drifting away from the anchored schooner. Gaston gasped and said, *"Mon Dieu! It's a woman! I can see her naked breasts!"*

Captain Gringo said, "It *was* a woman, you mean. Those bastards have enslaved both men and women. You still say it's not our fight?"

Gaston said, "We live in an unjust world, Dick. I have heard many of the *perleros* are girl divers. I agree we just saw a very ugly thing, but the smart move would be to get our derrieres out of here. Those men out there are *tres* casual about killing. They have a steel hull as well as modern weapons. Our Maxim slugs would do little more than dent their sides. If they use their diesel engine to move in on us, shooting back, from behind steel bulwarks, ohh, la! la!"

The crewman they'd sent for the machine gun returned with another. They were packing the Maxim and ammo boxes between them on their hands and knees. One of them asked, "What happened? We heard shots."

Captain Gringo said, "Keep your heads and voices down. I'll fill you in later."

As he started to set the Maxim up over a fallen log, the men aboard the schooner were shouting out across the water and the dark heads were moving toward the craft. There was a ladder off the stern and as the first captive diver climbed timidly up it, Gaston said, "Look! That one is a female, too, and very nicely built."

Captain Gringo pulled back on the arming lever and elevated his muzzle as he asked, "Still want to leave them to the mercy of those rats?"

"Ah, well, one must be *practique,* but maidens in distress are another matter. How are we to get the whites without killing the Indians, though?"

"That's a good question."

One of the white men aboard the schooner had a big black whip in his hand and as the Indian girl came aboard he flattened her to the deck with a brutal slash. Captain Gringo said, "There's the answer," and opened fire.

He'd aimed a bit high in his anxiety about the captive divers still in the water, so his first burst hit the main mast above the slaver's heads and showered them with splinters. He followed the mast down to splatter the man with the whip to bloody hash before he swung his barrel right to sweep the gun crew. They were good. They hadn't panicked. They were swinging the Gatling's multiple muzzle his way as he ranged on them, stopped long enough to steady his aim, and opened up again. He blew the gunner away from the breech and the loader dove off the stern in panic as a man in a striped shirt popped out of the cabin, waving a rifle and shouting in confusion. Captain Gringo nailed him to the cabin wall with a burst of slugs and stopped, ears ringing, to search for more targets. The man who'd thought he was diving to safety had made a grim mistake. The Indian girls in the water closed in on him, screaming like fishwives. They'd been given lengths of scrap iron to pry the oysters off the banks below. The resulting water fight looked like someone had had spilled a bottle of catsup in boiling water.

Something funny was going on aboard the mystery vessel. Another man popped out a hatch, but before Captain Gringo could fire he, too, dove headlong over the side. A skinny figure in white ducks followed to the rail, waving a big stick. Gaston said, "Shoot!" but Captain Gringo said, "I don't think so. I don't think that guy's on their side."

A couple of stark naked Indian girls came out to join the skinny guy and all three moved aft to shout down to the girls in the water. One of them came up the ladder and pointed their way. So Captain Gringo rose to his feet, breaking cover, and waved. The skinny guy waved back. Gaston pleaded, "Get down, you maniac! You've exposed our position and they still have that Gatling gun!"

The tall American said, "They're not moving to man the gun. A couple of them seem to be breaking out a dinghy. Just stay cool and let's hear what they have to say. I think the war is over."

So they watched and waited as a couple of Indian

girls lowered the little dinghy and got into it with the white guy in the white ducks. As they paddled over, Captain Gringo studied the unexpected visitor. He was about Gaston's height, but built like a kid. He had flaming red hair and a handsome teen-aged face. Neither he nor the two naked girls paddling the dinghy had thought to pack sidearms. So as they approached. Captain Gringo moved to the water's edge to grab their painter. The red-headed youth leaped ashore and held out a hand, saying, "Mac-Tavish, here, and in your debt, whoever ye be."

MacTavish had a thick Scottish brogue and they were near the old Highland colony he'd heard about, but it was impolite to ask too many questions in these parts, so Captain Gringo just shook hands and said, "I'm Dick Walker. My friends and I noticed somebody was shooting girls out of season, so . . ."

"Ay, ye came just in time," MacTavish cut in, adding. "They had me in irons. But when the shooting started a couple of the lasses set me free and ye know the rest."

"I do?"

"Och, were ye nae sent by my people to rescue me and me crew?"

"Mr. MacTavish, I have no idea what you're talking about. We're off a salted-up steam vessel and we came here looking for water. We saw what was going on and we didn't like it much. So what the hell has been going on?"

MacTavish grinned and said, "Och, ye're even better Christians than I took ye for. Yon schooner is the *Thistle-gorm,* out of Dunuraba. She's a pearler, as ye may have guessed, and yon lassies are me crew."

"You're the skipper? You seem cheerful as hell, considering."

"Och, those pirates took us captive almost a week ago. It's me own fault. Athair told me never to talk to strangers, but when I saw a whaleboat adrift and flying distress signals . . ."

"Right. They didn't show you that Gatling gun until it was too late, huh?"

"Ay, I thought such piracy was a thing of the past, too. But their leader was Irish, a retarded race dwelling

124

in the past. They commandeered me vessel and the things they've been doing to me lassies is too shocking to talk about. The only reason they kept me alive was because none of them knew how to run me diesel. But all's well that ends well and, thanks to ye, I've come out of it pearls ahead. There's something to be said for pointing guns at pearl divers. I fear I've been a wee bit soft on me lassies."

Gaston came over, dubiously, and Captain Gringo introduced them. The youthful MacTavish said, "Neither of ye will leave here empty-handed. I've no money to give ye, but I'll split such pearls as we have aboard and ye'll be welcome to the pirates' Gatling gun if ye'll be kind enough to take it with ye."

Captain Gringo said, "We can use it. But keep your pearls. What we're really looking for is fresh water."

"Och, there's all ye want, just up the river a wee ways. How far is ye're stranded steamboat?"

"Three or four miles. We're hard aground, too."

"Ay, it's easy to do that, in these waters. Here's what MacTavish will do. We'll all go together up the river and we'll fill *Thistlegorm*'s tanks with water for yer poor boilers. Then we'll pop around to pump it aboard for ye. Thanks to Herr Diesel, *Thistlegorm*'s a handy craft."

Captain Gringo laughed and said, "I know. We tangled with you the other day. You took off like a loon with a rocket up its ass."

"Och, was that ye in that gunboat? I'm glad ye didn't sink us!"

"So am I, now. We'll move our own launch around this spit and tie up to your stern. We'll fill our own casks while we're at it. But I'm afraid it's going to take more than one trip."

"No matter. Me and the lassies are completely at yer service."

Gaston nudged Captain Gringo and winked as Mac-Tavish moved back to his dinghy. Captain Gringo had noticed the nice brown bodies, too, but he didn't wink back. He said, "We've got to suggest some clothes or something before the rest of our crew sees all that ass. God knows when some of them have had any, and I want to keep this kid on our side."

16

It actually would have taken three trips, if there'd been time. But as *Thistlegorm* was pumping the second load of fresh water aboard *La Tortuga,* the lookout in *La Tortuga*'s crow's nest reported smoke on the horizon. At the same time, Porter came out of the radio shack and ran to the rail to shout down at Captain Gringo, aboard *Thistlegorm,* "Just picked up a message in English. Remember that cruiser? Well, she's coming back!"

Gaston was standing between Captain Gringo and young MacTavish, holding the hose between vessels. He said, *"Merde alors!* They may miss spotting our camouflaged cripple again, but they can hardly miss this schooner! We'd better split up. *Thistlegorm* can duck back up the river long before the cruiser spots her."

Captain Gringo said, "I've got a better idea. MacTavish, your engine doesn't throw a smoke plume. How fast can you run her?"

"Och, twenty knocks, if I have to."

"You'll have to. Gaston, what's the maximum range of our four-inchers, at full elevation?"

"Three or four miles, perhaps. But one can't hope to hit anything at that range."

"You don't have to hit it. The cruiser's way around that bend over there, and moving slow. I want you to lob a couple of rounds in her general direction, when I'm ready."

"Dick, we are stuck in the mud with our engines

126

down. That cruiser has eight-inch guns. An eight-inch shell is not *twice* as big as a four-incher. It's *four times* as big! They can fire four times as far, too."

"Hell, everybody knows that."

"Then why on earth do you wish to attract attention to us with badly aimed and most pathetic fire?"

"I don't intend to draw attention to *La Tortuga*. I want to draw it *away* from her. We'll put a steel drum filled wth oily rags in a lifeboat we can spare and light a smudge fire. Then we'll lob a couple of rounds to let them know there's a four-inch gun in the general vicinity of the smoke they see over the trees."

MacTavish laughed and said, "Och, I see the cunning in the plan, Dick! We'll dash off, hugging yon shoreline as we trail the smoke on a long line, and yon cruiser will follow us as a mad dog chases a wee kitty!"

"Not without *me,* you won't!" said Gaston. "I'll fire the thrice-accursed guns, but then I intend to evacuate my derriere *tres* suddenly."

Captain Gringo said, "We'll take *all* our people off aboard *Thistlegorm*. If it doesn't work, the cruiser will blow *La Tortuga* to scrap and then make nails and bailing wire out of her. How far up that river can you go, MacTavish?"

"A lot farther than any cruiser, I'll vow."

"Okay, we'll cast off the smoke pot on the far side and double back. But we've talked enough. Let's move our tails. Have you been thinking about my suggestions regarding your nubile maidens, Mac?"

MacTavish nodded and said, "Ay, they're to wear feed sacks and try to stay pure. But, as I told ye, me lassies can take care of themselves. They're jungle-bred and inclined to be athletic with a would-be rapist."

"I saw what they did to those pirates in the water. But I don't want us fighting among ourselves. We've got enough trouble. Gaston, get on that gun like I told you. I'll see to the smudge pot."

Six nautical miles away, *H.M.S. Dunraven* was moving slowly and majestically toward the narrow passage between the bend in the shores and the deserted Malata on her starboard. Ensign Forsythe was watching for the mysterious outline he'd noted before. It should be coming up, just beyond the narrows. From the crow's nest high above, he heard the shout of, "Smoke ahead! Two points off the port bow!"

Forsythe raised his binoculars and murmured to the skipper at his side, "I see it, sir. I'd say there's a steam vessel just around that point."

The skipper said, "I'm hardly blind, dear boy. She's seen our plume, too. She's dead in the water. We'll soon know who she is."

There was a high-pitched whistle, somewhere in the sky, and both looked up, squinting into the glare. Then a geyser of spray rose a quarter mile away, followed within seconds by the dull boom of high explosives detonating under water. Forsythe gasped, "I say!" but the skipper wasn't listening; he was running with surprising speed for a man his age. He dashed into the wheelhouse and told the startled watch commander, "Full speed ahead," as he reached for his telephone. The skipper cranked the handle hard and once as he shouted into the mouthpiece, *"Answer* me, goddamn your eyes!"

"Fire Control," replied a calmer voice in his ear. The skipper glanced through the windscreen as another shell landed, dead ahead, and demanded, "Haven't you noticed we're under fire, you moron?"

"Waiting orders, sir."

"Well, you *have* your perishing orders, damn your eyes! Range on that bloody smoke and blow it out of the bloody water!"

The fire control officer had been readier than his calm voice might have indicated. *H.M.S. Dunraven* tingled all over and sat back on her stern as the forward turret let fly a salvo of fire and steel with a mighty roar. The view forward was momentarily blocked by a huge cloud of pungent cordite smoke, then, as *H.M.S. Dunraven* tore forward through it, the skipper shouted into the telephone, "She's still moving and still afloat, goddamn it! I told you to range on her, not to throw snowballs! You're over or under, you stupid young twit!"

The fore guns fired again without comment, and this time they moved through their own smoke faster. There was a rainbow hanging between them and the smoke above the trees of the bend, now. The skipper didn't think it was pretty. They'd obviously blown a lot of water into the sunlit sky. He had something else in mind. The damned smoke plume of the other vessel was still brazenly moving, and rather fast. As they tore through the passage, it was ducking around another bloody point. The blighters were hugging the coastline. The skipper yelled, "Fire! Damn it!" and his guns obeyed.

Young Forsythe ran in off the wing to shout, "I think I saw that gunboat again, sir."

"Of course you saw it, you perishing idiot! It just nipped around that point ahead!"

"Nossir. We just *passed* it! It's against the shoreline, dead in the water. I had a better look at it, this time, and I'm sure it's a camouflaged vessel, painted with grey and green stripes."

The watch commander stepped over quietly and said, "We're almost to speed, sir. But may I point out we're in a treacherous channel?"

"God strike a bloody light! They've fired on Her Majesty's colors! Can't either of you understand a simple order? Look out that bloody windscreen, both of you, and tell me what you see!"

The watch commander said, "It's a steamer plume, of course, sir. She's around the bend and hugging the shore. We know she doesn't have our draft. We have to swing wider."

"I don't give a ruddy fuck *how* we take the turn, damn it! Just get me and my guns *around* it!"

Forsythe said, "Sir, that camouflaged vessel we just passed . . ." and the skipper exploded, "Get off my bridge, you near-sighted maniac! I don't care what you think you saw. I *know* those shells came at us from whoever is steaming just ahead of us at flank speed. I'm not at all interested in any other bloody boats at the moment."

"But, sir . . ."

"I said to get off me bridge! Another word and I'll have you in irons!"

As the ensign scurried to get out of the old man's

angry glare the skipper yelled into the phone, "What are you waiting for, an engraved invitation? Fire at will until I tell you to stop, goddamn it to hell!"

And so, guns blazing and moving with a bone in her teeth, *H.M.S. Dunraven* tore up the channel after the teasing smoke plume until, of course, the inevitable happened.

The skipper was thrown to the deck as the foreguns fired and for a moment he thought the recoil had knocked his legs out from under him. But as the watch commander helped him to his feet, the older man frowned and said, "I say, we don't seem to be moving very fast."

"We're not moving at all, sir. We've run aground."

The skipper took off his hat, threw it on the deck, and kicked it before he turned to stare out the windscreen. The distant smoke plume was still there, albeit fading and moving more to seaward. The bridge phone rang. It was Fire Control. They wanted to know if they should fire again at this range. The old man said, "No. Carry on." Then he hung up, turned to the watch officer, and said, "Tell Sparks to see if he can raise *H.M.S. Ashton* and tell them the pirates are headed back toward Chagres."

"Ay ay, sir. Shall we inform them we're aground?"

"You do and I'll have your balls for supper! *R.N.* does not run aground. We simply seem to have a reef stuck to our keel at the moment. We'll get off ourselves, if it takes us until 1900. Just tell Ashton the blighters are a bit faster and shallower draft than we were told."

17

By sundown *La Tortuga*'s engines were running again, more or less. Gaston would have preferred a more thorough rinsing and general overhaul, but he was particular about what sort of wine he had with fish, given any choice.

There wasn't any choice. The cruiser had chased their barrel of burning rags somewhere, but there was no way of knowing it was gone for good. So with the willing help of MacTavish and the Indian pearl divers, they ran out the kedge lines and as soon as the sky was safely dark, fired up the boilers. MacTavish helped by using the shallow-draft *Thistlegorm* as a diesel tug, and as all hands worked together, *La Tortuga* slowly hauled herself out of the thin sticky mud until her screws were free. The two vessels then made for the river estuary, *Thistlegorm* politely slowed for the awkward and strangely painted gunboat. At Captain Gringo's orders, most of the guerrillas and deserters were back aboard *La Tortuga*. They'd been too busy, up to now, for trouble to arise between the oddly mismatched crews, but he'd noticed the looks his men were giving the Indian girls. MacTavish had them all wearing something, but they were shapely from their swimming and too simple to ignore a grinning sailor or fend off a lewd remark with a cool comment any Hispanic girl could have managed.

MacTavish struck him as pretty innocent, too. The kid had adopted them with no apparent reservations and

131

couldn't seem to understand that a navy deserter might not be a man you'd trust with a teen-aged jungle girl. Captain Gringo hadn't had a time to size MacTavish up until, up the uncharted river and around a couple of bends, the two craft anchored side by side and there was time to talk. MacTavish had the Indian girls cleaning up the *Thistlegorm* as Captain Gringo came aboard. The gunfire hadn't done any structural damage to speak of. But they had to clean off all the blood and crud before they patched and painted.

The invitation to supper had only been extended to the three "white men" aboard *La Tortuga*. Catalina O'Hara and at least six or seven of the others were as white as MacTavish, but it was his vessel, so what the hell. Gaston wanted to stay aboard *La Tortuga* and fuss with both her guns and engines some more. Porter was picking up all sorts of interesting stuff on the Marconi set and it was agreed at least one of them should stay on the bridge. So the tall American ate alone with MacTavish.

The meal was served in the main cabin by naked Indian ladies and Captain Gringo was half finished before he noticed he was eating "Moors and Christians," the ubiquitous beans and rice dish of Latin America. MacTavish seemed oblivious of the nicely stacked young native girls, so Captain Gringo assumed he'd had them both. He'd probably had them all. MacTavish drank heartily as they shared Moors and Christians, and few skippers of an all-female crew could miss the obvious advantages, cold sober. It was no wonder the kid was skinny. The American was too polite to ask MacTavish his age, so he made an educated guess or two, revising it upwards as MacTavish talked. The guy had been too many places and done too many things to be the teen-ager he appeared. Captain Gringo decided he was one of those androgynous little guys who never wound up with much hair on their chests. He hoped that was all. As they worked on the bottle that went with the meal, MacTavish took to shooting odd looks his way and asking rather pointed questions about his visitor's sex life.

Like most men, Captain Gringo had met his share

of homosexuals. But he hadn't been propositioned often since he'd started shaving. He was too sure of his own manhood to have to prove it by bulging muscles at anyone, but most of them seemed aware he was a lost cause and tended to leave him alone. MacTavish was starting to make him nervous. He wasn't afraid the little guy would ravage him, but he really wasn't up to any more dumb conversations and hurt looks. He'd only come to dinner to avoid that aboard *La Tortuga*. Cielita was still flirting with him and Cathy seemed to expect him to drag her into any hidden corner they could manage. He was still trying to think up a graceful way to drop her. She might get sore if he said he wanted out. Her husband, General Puma, was going to be even more so, if he found out, and he would, if they kept the affair going.

He steered the conversation with MacTavish into calmer waters by asking questions about the pearler's past. It would have been more interesting if MacTavish hadn't drawn his legs up elfinly on the built-in couch and batted his eyelashes like that. The jug on the table was some kind of moonshine MacTavish said they made back home, and while it went down pretty smooth, MacTavish couldn't hold it worth a damn. It was hard enough to understand a guy with a brogue. A drunk who giggled and slurred a brogue was even worse.

Thistlegorm was out of Port Uruba in the Gulf of Darien. The schooner was new. MacTavish had gone to Kiel, Germany, to pick her up and sail her back. He'd gotten to Kiel, along with his all-girl crew, aboard the vessel of a clansman, and the two vessels had separated on the way back. Captain Gringo asked how the Germans had reacted to the naked Indian pearl divers and Mac-Tavish winked and said, "Awheel, we made the lassies wear mother hubbards, but yon Dutchmen did give us funny looks. My clansman, Ian Og, said I was daft to race him home wi' naught but lassies and an untried diesel. But we left him hull down over the horizon the first day out and we'd have been in Port Uruba this nicht if we hadn't been boarded by pirates. But, thanks to ye and yer shooting, we'll all be there safe and sound, save one."

MacTavish stared into the amber contents of the

133

jug and sighed softly before adding, "I'll see the dead lassie's family will get her share and more, but I dinna ken how I'm to break such news to the wee savages."

"I know the feeling. Where is this Port Uruba, Mac? I've been studying the charts of these waters pretty good in the last few days and Uruba doesn't ring any bells."

MacTavish said, "Och, we're on no map. Who wants to pay taxes? Our settlement is all that's left of a grand daft scheme. We were chartered by the Scottish Parliament in 1695. I fear most of the settlers who came over didna make it, but our group were fisherfolk from the West Highlands. So we made no effort to grow oats and potatoes in the jungle and . . ."

"Just a minute," Captain Gringo cut in with a puzzled frown, "I've heard of the Darien Scheme. It was a total disaster. Those poor Scots were almost wiped out by the Indians and fever and the few who lived went home."

MacTavish said, "Not *all* of them. I said my kinsmen were fisherfolk. The sea is the sea to a man who kens her ways and nae man who's sailed the raw cruel waters of the North Atlantic can be drowned in the tepid calms of the Caribbean. We'd settled in a healthy cove and made friends with the Indians, who were sea folk like our ain sels. When Scotland gave up the idea of a colony over here, they neglected to tell us, and the others left without us."

The American laughed and said, "It sounds like Rip Van Winkle. But, come to think of it, there *are* some Dutch-speaking villages left in upstate New York, today. But doesn't the Colombian government know you're there?"

"Och, I sincerely hope not! Ye see, the old Spanish rule of the isthmus left a wee bit to be desired, we being Protestants and as set in our ways as they were in theirs. Fortunately, nobody kens much about the Darien jungle and nobody who has no friends among the Indians can get far into it. When Colombia got her freedom from Spain we saw no reason to pester them with applications to pay taxes or take out fishing licenses. If they don't bother us, we won't bother them."

134

The American took another sip of his drink and said, "Great. This is the break I've been looking for. If we can all get to your jungle hide-out, we'll be safe."

MacTavish looked dubious and said, "Awheel, I'm sure ye and yon French and American friends would be welcome. Ye did save me and *Thistlegorm*. But I dinna ken about the others. They're Panamanians."

"Sure, but they're rebels. They're not from the government. They're *against* the government."

"Ay, they are *noo*. But what if they *win,* some day?"

"Hmm, you've got a point there, Mac. But, hell, you hold-out Scotch colonists can't really expect to be forgotten forever in your jungle, can you?"

"Not forever. But nobody's bothered us since 1699. That's almost two hundred years. We're in nae hurry to be found. It wouldna frush us if they left us alone another hundred or so."

"Come on, Mac. With all the interest in the projected Panaman Canal, this corner of the world is going to be important. Somebody has to stumble over you. I doubt it'll be far from the turn of the century. If I were you, I'd be trying to make friends among the Panamanians. They're bound to wind up in charge down here, sooner or later."

MacTavish took another belt, swallowed, and said, "Ay, but yer nae me, and I'm nae Athair."

"Athair?"

"That's father, in the Gaelic. My father is the Mac-Tavish of Uruba. What ye sassenach call a chief. We've all been raised by Athair to tell nae outsiders the way to Port Uruba."

MacTavish took another drink and added, "On the other hand, we've been raised never to turn our backs on a man who does us a good turn, and the turn ye did with yon machine gun was a bonny one indeed. Ye can see the pickle ye have me in, Dick Walker. I owe ye, but I wish there was some other way to pay ye back."

The tall American was uncomfortably aware that MacTavish was staring thoughtfully at his fly as he said that. The little red-headed Scot was drunk as a skunk and looking downright amorous as he added, "Och, we'll

135

figure something out in the morning. I'm for going off to bed. How about ye, Dick Walker?"

"Uh, yeah, I guess I'll head back to *La Tortuga* and get some shut-eye."

"Will ye, noo? Which one's eyes have ye been shutting, Dick? The Spanish lass or the wee *mestiza's?*"

"I was wondering if you'd noticed Cathy or Cielita, Mac." The American grinned, relieved to reestablish his sexual preferences.

MacTavish shrugged and said, "I tried a girl, once. A bawdy lass from our village said she had a way of pleasing that we'd keep our own wee secret. I didn't enjoy it."

"Gee, I'm sorry to hear that, Mac. But I've never had any trouble that way. You might say I'm sort of queer for women. No offense."

MacTavish grimaced and said, "Ay, I figured as much. But ye dinna have to go back to yon gunboat if that's all that's drawing ye from my side. I'm sure we can make ye comfortable, here aboard *Thistlegorm,* and, well, to tell the truth, I'd feel safer if ye stayed aboard with us for the nicht. Some of those Panamanian men are sort of big and . . ."

"I can post a guard," he cut in.

"Ay, but who's to guard the guard, once ye're oot of sight and oot of mind? Won't ye stay the nicht, Dick?"

"Mac, I'm trying to think of a nice way to say this, but it wouldn't work. I mean, I like you, but not enough to sleep with you."

MacTavish looked hurt and said, "Ay, I thought ye preferred the great rump of yon *mestiza*. Or is it the tits of yon Spanish lass ye've such a fancy for?"

"Let's keep it friendly, Mac. You have your preferences and I have mine. As a matter of fact, I was planning to sleep alone. But since you brought it up, I'm afraid I'll have to admit I'm an unreconstructed tits-and-fanny man."

"Ay, just my luck I had to find a meat-and-potatoes primitive so attractive. But I'm fair drunk and so I'll not try to convince ye ye might be missing the finer things in life."

"I'm not trying to convince you that your way is

wrong, either. So do we part friends? Frankly, I'm glad we got it out in the open."

MacTavish shrugged and said, "Och, I *must* be drunk. But I'm glad ye know how I feel and we'll say nae more about it. But if ye don't fancy sleeping with *me,* could I induce ye to stay aboard anyway? More than one of my Indian lassies would be pleased to make ye comfortable. They've been at sea a while and they're bonny bawdy wenches. I've two in the crew who've gotten so wild they even try to get at me. Do ye want to choose between them or shall I send them *both* to yer cabin?"

"Jesus, you're sort of tempting me, Mac."

"Ay, that was my intention. I dinna want ye to leave. I was hoping ye'd be willing to overlook the anatomical problems ye might have been nice enough to overlook. But if ye don't want me, there's plenty of the usual stuff aboard *Thistlegorm* and I believe in hospitality."

Captain Gringo hesitated. MacTavish looked up pleadingly and murmured, "Stay, Dick. If nae as a lover, stay as a friend."

"Well, shit, since you put it that way . . ."

18

So Captain Gringo stayed aboard *Thistlegorm* for the night, but he didn't get much sleep. MacTavish showed him to a small cabin and said good night with a wistful sigh. The two Indian girls joined him within minutes, stark naked and giggling a lot. One had a pretty face with Caucasian features. The other was pure moon-faced Carib with eyes like a cat and a short stocky frame that bulged pure female no matter where you touched it, and he had to. She introduced herself by taking his hand and placing it on her firm mahogany breast as the other one unbuckled their guest's belt. They were both toasted browner than many a Negress by the sea and sun and they smelled like what they were—two pretty little animals who probably didn't know what soap was, but were clean enough to eat off, thanks to all the swimming they'd had.

Neither seemed to feel formality was called for, but as they got him on the bunk and proceeded to shuck him like an ear of corn, he established that the pretty one was called XiXi, which was sort of hard to pronounce, and her moon-faced companion said to call her Xoxocatl, which he wasn't about to try. Neither spoke Spanish worth a damn. It saved a lot of questions. He knew what they'd come for and they knew he knew. So he started to kiss and fondle XiXi as Xoxocatl finished pulling his socks off. The next thing he knew he was flat on his back with XiXi's nipple in his mouth and one of them, he didn't know which, on his shaft and going crazy. He felt a little crazy, too. Her clean tight love box moved as if it hadn't had a man for months, which was probably true. XiXi giggled something in her jungle dialect and started moving up toward the head of the bunk. As he kissed her brown belly he realized he had to be screwing the moon-faced Xoxocatl, or maybe it was the other way around, since he was pinned down and she was moving like spit on a hot stove.

He didn't speak Carib, but he knew what XiXi expected from him as she placed a brown thigh on either side of his head and tried to raise his face with her caressing hands. He said, "I hardly know you, honey, but if you're sure this is your first trick, tonight . . ."

XiXi didn't understand and wouldn't have gotten it if she had. She thrust her pelvis teasingly at his face and he noticed, by the dim light, that, like most Indians, she'd plucked out all the hairs between her legs. He took a deep breath and accepted her genital kiss, teasing her aroused pink clit with his tongue as, meanwhile, he felt himself coming in the other one.

It felt wild as hell to eat pussy with an Indian war dance going on at the other end.

The American knew his host, MacTavish, had to be hearing what was going on, unless he'd jumped overboard. Mac's cabin was right across the companionway and there were jalousies for ventilation in the cabin doors. So he kept his own noise down. But then XiXi started hollering and trying to pull his head inside her. He put two fingers in her as he went on tonguing. XiXi started to contract around them as Xoxocatl did the same around his shaft and he was trying to decide which one had the nicest interior as he enjoyed a long shuddering orgasm. The warm gusher inside her seemed to delight Xoxocatl, but he was sort of embarrassed by her vocal comments on it. He didn't speak her dialect, but he knew MacTavish did. He felt sorry for the poor little swish. MacTavish was a nice guy and it probably wasn't his fault that he was queer. Captain Gringo had never understood how a well-hung regular guy could get his jollies off with a man, but he'd read somewhere that certain boys were born with undecided glands. Mac probably felt like a woman in a man's body. He'd sure as hell started to act like one with a few drinks in him.

The girls decided to change places. He didn't seem to have much to say about it. XiXi hadn't come, yet, and she must have preferred the real thing, because the next thing he knew she'd shoved Xoxocatl off and was screwing herself onto him. He'd been right. She was tighter as well as prettier, and his virile member rose to the new challenge.

But he didn't really want to taste his own semen all that much, so he rolled XiXi over and mounted her right before XoXocatl could sit on his face. She grabbed one of his hands and began to masturbate herself with it, sitting cross-legged with her back against the bulkhead as she watched the two of them go at it, grinning as though she enjoyed the show. He found that a nice distraction, too, and proceeded to ravage Xoxocatl with his fist as he laid XiXi. XiXi was a born contortionist, as well as tightly built. She got her thighs between them and locked her ankles around his neck to help him bounce while he worked three fingers into Xoxocatl and, since she seemed to want more, hooked a pinky up her anus. She like that, too. He could tell she was coming, and XiXi joined her as they both yelled how good they felt.

He held back, or tried to, but it was too exciting a scene, and he ruined XiXi as an item fit for human consumption by filling her to overflowing. She coyly informed her friend of this and it seemed they wanted to switch again. He was willing. But he didn't know how long he could keep this up. Either of the primitive little nymphomaniacs would have been more than enough for one man and one night. Captain Gringo didn't consider himself a sissy. He'd met few women he couldn't sate. More than one had begged for mercy in his time. But these two were not only hot-natured, they were trained athletes with tireless swimmer's muscles and lungs. He grinned wryly as he thought how he'd offered to protect Mac's female crew from being ravaged. These two, alone, could probably take on every man aboard *La Tortuga* and ask for second helpings!

So, it was tough about old Mac. They needed to

stay on the good side of him. That hide-out in Port Uruba sounded great. But Mac's ideas on sex just weren't his cup of tea. He knew he couldn't get it up with a guy if it meant it would save his life. His *brain* could see the sense of it. The Lord knew he'd made love to some ugly broads in the past to save his ass. But his shaft, he knew, would betray him. He was going limp, just thinking about it, in the middle of having a woman.

So, putting the odd thoughts out of his mind, he concentrated on what he was doing to Xoxocatl, and Xoxocatl responded with renewed vigor of her own. But he really didn't start to enjoy it again until he saw little XiXi was coming, rolled the bawdy Xoxocatl aside, and mounted XiXi to do it right. As he entered her, normally, XiXi enveloped him in smooth salty female flesh and crooned something husky in his ear as she chewed it. He said, "Yeah, coming, mother. It's the only way to finish, once you get past the trimmings."

19

He didn't have to face MacTavish in the cold gray light of dawn. He crawled back aboard *La Tortuga* before the little Scot was up. He'd had maybe an hour's sleep and more screwing than any sensible man felt the need of.

He went aboard unchallenged. There was supposed to be a deck watch. But they were up the river and, what the hell, if the sailors had been interested in their duties they might never have deserted.

He took a shower and let himself into his own cabin. He found Cathy O'Hara waiting there for him. She had on a kimono and was perched on his bunk, reading and smoking. He could see by the contents of his ash tray that she'd been waiting a while.

She said, "Deek, I think I am falling in love with you, but I have a terrible confession to make."

He had some confessions to make, too, but he decided to let her go first. His shirt was already unbuttoned. He took it off and sat down beside her. She said, "Wait. I did not come here to make love. After I tell you what I must, you may not wish to make love to me ever again. I have been very bad. But the other night I lost my head. There was no time for me to explain before it was too late for both of us."

"We lost our heads," he agreed, slipping an arm around her waist. He doubted he could get it up at gun point, right now, but if he went through the motions she expected of him, maybe somebody would ring the breakfast gong or something.

Cathy put a hand on his wrist and said, "Wait, darling. You know I want to, but we have for to talk. You see, I am not free."

"No shit? How much do you charge?" he grinned.

"Stop teasing. If you must know, I am a married woman."

"Who asked? Why must I know? You're not married to anyone around here, are you?"

She sighed and said, "No. My husband is a leader of the Liberation movement. It is this, more than anything else, that has me so confused. I know you both love me. But Benito needs me."

He took his hand away and reached for a smoke. Cathy moved closer to him, allowing her kimono to gap alarmingly for a renunciation scene. She said, "I see I have hurt you, dear. But we must be brave. The reason you attract me is that you are, well, stronger than Benito. He is *muy toro* and a very noisy fighter. But, under all his bluster he is still a boy."

Captain Gringo shrugged. He didn't know how else to answer.

She said, "Yes, I confess it. I wish for to stay with you and make love forever. But I am a patriot as well as a woman in love. It is all so confusing. Can I put my own desires above the liberation of my country?"

Again he shrugged and tried, "Can't old Benito find another gal?"

"Of course. General Puma is most popular with the ladies. But that is not the problem. You see, my husband is a good fighter and an acceptable lover. But he is not very bright."

"You mean you've been doing his thinking as well as his laundry?"

"Somebody has to. Benito's idea of a revolution is to wrap himself in the rebel flag and charge with a gun in each hand."

"Ouch. I know the type. I can see why the Colombian military police picked you up. What you're trying to tell me is that you have to go back to Benito to save the revolution as well as his hide, right?"

She sighed wistfully and replied, "His hide no longer holds as much attraction for me as it once did. But yes, I owe it to my country to make certain sacrifices."

She dabbed a tear from her eye and said, "Oh, I knew you would be big about it and that makes it even harder for me. How can we ever part, Dick?"

"It won't be easy. But that's life. I'm trying to get us to a safe place where we can sweat out the chase until it cools off. Once the authorities are no longer in hot pursuit, it shouldn't be hard for you to make your way back to the rebel lines."

"Won't you be coming with me, Dick? Benito could use a machine gunner."

"I'd love to be coming with you. But it wouldn't work."

"Ah, the thought of me in another man's arms would drive you mad with jealousy, no?"

"That's close enough. A clean break is best in situations like these."

Cathy let her kimono fall all the way open as she said, "Well, I'm glad we have an understanding. We agree to give this madness up, but we don't have to be *silly* about it, eh?"

"Honey, I wish you'd make up your mind."

"I have, dear. I must go back to Benito, once the coast is, how you say, clear? But, meanwhile. . ."

He shook his head and said, "I don't think we'd better. I said it's best to break clean."

"But, Dick, it may be *weeks* before it's safe for me to return to my husband."

"Yeah, it's going to be hard on both of us. But . . ." And then she was groping at his fly and purring, "I know it will be hard. I like it hard, you brute."

He felt a tingle he hadn't really ever expected to feel again as she rose from the bunk to straddle his knees with her open thighs, giving him a close-up view of her swaying breasts as she bent to unbutton his pants. It was tempting as hell. But as long as he'd been screwed blue, he might as well take advantage of it to be sensible. He shook his head and pleaded, "Don't tease me, Cathy. I don't think I could ever let you go if we went any further."

"Just a little quick one, before breakfast?"

"I want to," he lied, "but we have to think of *La Revolucion*."

"Oh, you are so strong! I have never met a man with so much control."

"It comes with clean living. You've got to hang tough, too, doll. If we give in to our desires there's no telling what will become of Panama."

She hesitated, thighs open in welcome and breathing hard, and it looked for a minute like her revolution was in trouble. Then they both heard somebody moving down the companionway outside and she, said, "Damn."

He said, "The ship's waking up. We'll talk some more about it later. But you've got to get out of here while there's still time. If anyone spots you coming from my quarters in that kimono there's no telling what will get back to your husband."

She got off him, saying, "Brrr! Benito can be cruel when he is aroused, and I would not want the two of you fighting over me."

He nodded and said, "Smart thinking. Right now I have to get up to the bridge."

So they parted friends, if not lovers. Cathy got to think of herself as a self-sacrificing heroine and Captain Gringo was saved a lot of explanations about his limp and wrung-out manhood, too, most likely.

He went outside and headed for the conning tower. At the base of the ladder he was stopped by Gomez and two other men. One was Angelo, the semi-leader of the guerrillas. The other was the self-appointed leader of the deserters, a big thug called Malo.

Gomez said, "Forgive us, Captain. We mean no disrespect. But the others have appointed us a delegation."

"*Et tu,* Gomez? Delegate away, then."

"Well, my Captain, the men have been wondering if there is some, uh, *plan* to all this nonsense."

Captain Gringo frowned and growled, "I'd hardly call it nonsense. You're all at liberty and still alive, which is a hell of an improvement over the way I found you!"

"*Es verdad,* and we are most grateful. But, forgive me, we do not seem to be *going* anywhere!"

The tall American nodded and said, "I'm aware of that. I'd take you all to Paris and let you see the cancan, if I could. But it's not up to me. The Colombian Army is searching for us by land and the Royal Navy by sea. Meanwhile we're up a creek with nothing *but* the paddles until we fix our cranky engines. Next question."

Malo said, "Hey, we got the engine running while you were playing with that fairy on the other boat all night."

Captain Gringo's fist was a blur as he planted a left cross in the middle of Malo's face. The big man's head thunked against the steel bulkhead behind him and he slid down it, bloody and glazed, to wind up sitting on the deck.

The others froze in place as Captain Gringo's .38 appeared as if by magic in his other hand. Gomez gulped and said, "*Ay que muchacho*! I said we meant no disrespect, my Captain!"

The tall American smiled pleasantly and replied, "I'm sure it was simply curiosity. But, for the record, Señor MacTavish and I are just good friends. As I was saying before this jerk-off spoke out of turn, my plan, such as it is, is to wait a day or so until the chase cools off. We've plenty of food and water. Nobody knows we're here, I hope. We've been intercepting wireless messages from that British cruiser and that gives us an advantage they don't know about. We'll know when they call off the search."

Angelo asked, "Where will we go, then, Señor?"

"Where do you want to go, Angelo? I haven't checked it out, yet, but I've heard there are some water routes across to the Pacific via the swamps of Darien. If MacTavish's Indians can show us a way to get this gunboat through, we'll surprise the shit out of a lot of people. If we can't do that, we're going to have to get another vessel and quietly double back to drop you guys off closer to home."

"We could take the *Thistlegorm,* no? She has papers and is not wanted anywhere as an outlaw."

Captain Gringo controlled his voice as he replied,

"There isn't much room for all of us aboard the schooner, even if you wanted to degenerate your revolution into simple piracy."

Angelo and Gomez exchanged glances. Then Gomez said, "There would be room, if we put Señor MacTavish and his female crew ashore. That Gatling gun on the *Thistlegorm,* in addition to our own Maxim, would leave us in possession of a swift, well-armed vessel. The world would be our oyster. We could go anywhere and do anything, with such a fine ship."

Captain Gringo shook his head and said, "You're not listening. I know there's a fine line between rebel and outlaw, but once you haul down the red flag and run up the black, you're a pirate for keeps. Even a free Panama would repudiate you. You'd never be able to go home again, no matter who wins the revolution."

Angelo shrugged and said, "Who has to go home, and to what? I have heard tales of the old pirate days and they sound like fun."

"Aw, shit, grow up. Morgan and Blackbeard went out of style a hundred years ago. It's almost the twentieth century."

"Some things never change, Señor."

"Bullshit. They have better communications, now, and if there's one thing every country agrees on today, it's that piracy is no longer in fashion. Don't you guys know anything about international law? During the War of 1812 British and American frigates hunted down pirates in pairs while their countries were at war! Let word get out that there's a motor-driven pirate vessel in these waters and every navy on earth will send ships to get in on the fun you mentioned. Hell, the Royal Navy will invite the Kaiser's ships to join in the hunt and I wouldn't be surprised if the Czar and the Sultan of Turkey could resist such a chance to try out their new ironclads."

"What about the Monroe Doctrine, Señor?"

"Yeah, what about it? Uncle Sam tends to worry about other powers moving in to grab *real estate* down here. There's nothing in the Monroe Doctrine meant to protect pirates. Forget it, *muchachos.* It just wouldn't work, even if I'd let you try, which I won't."

147

The groggy Malo on the deck raised a hand to his face, stared in wonder at the blood, and muttered, "Hey, somebody *hit* me!"

Captain Gringo nodded and said, "Yeah. You had it coming. Where did you get so interested in sodomy, Malo? I've heard about you sailor boys."

"I'll get you for this," Malo growled.

"No you won't," smiled Captain Gringo, pleasantly. He added. "You got off lightly, I guess I'm just an easygoing slob. But I'd watch that mouth, if I were you. A lot of guys would have killed you for calling them a fairy. Telling me you're going to get me while you're on your ass with a bloody nose and I'm standing over you with a gun is *really* pressing your luck!" He turned to Gomez and said, "You'd better take him somewhere and cool him off. A guy that stupid really needs a keeper."

Gomez said, "He is just excited, my Captain. We won't let him hurt you."

"Gee, that's big of you, Gomez. I've got to get topside. Tell the others we're going to shelter here for the day at least. If Gaston says *La Tortuga* is up to a sea run, and that fucking cruiser isn't watching the mouth of this river, we may make a run for Darien tonight."

Then, not waiting to see if they had any other questions or complaints, he went up into the conning tower.

The wheelhouse was deserted. But Porter heard him and came out of the radio shack. Porter said, "Goddamned batteries are fading on me. Where have you been?"

"Just fucking around. What do you mean the batteries are fading? We've got extra acid, haven't we?"

"Sure, but that's not the problem. The zinc plates in the jars should have been replaced some time ago. I've looked all over, and I can't find any goddamned spare plates."

"That figures. The old crew hasn't fixed a thing since they got this tub from the Brits. Are you picking up anything at all?"

"Yeah. That's why I'm worried about the batteries. That cruiser is sending, not too far from here. They say they think we've moved up the coast. But *they're* not moving. They might know we've got a Marconi set aboard."

Captain Gringo nodded and said, "Yeah. Could be a ruse, at that. So much for a daylight run. We'll stay here until after sundown, at least. Then, if they haven't sent marines up the river, we'll know they're just guessing we're around here *some* damned place. We'll wait 'til they give up and . . ."

"Dick, I'm trying to get through to you, but you're someplace else. It won't matter what they send or receive in a little while. I can barely hear them, now."

"How do you know they're holding still, then? Couldn't the signals be fading because they've moved off?"

"No. Two reasons. They just said they'd taken up a position at anchor to inspect the bilges or something. They were kind of coy about just why they'd stopped. The second reason is chemistry. The plates are so corroded I wouldn't be able to pick up anything if they weren't close as hell."

Captain Gringo went over his own high school chemistry in his head as he frowned and said, "Hmmm, we need to know. The battery plates are zinc and copper, right?"

Porter nodded and said, "Of course. The copper plates have held up pretty good. But the zinc ones are paper-thin and full of holes."

"Okay, as I understand basic electronics, the current is produced by two different metals immersed in an acid bath. We'd get a weak current from iron and copper, so there goes my tin can idea. How about silver?"

Porter nodded and said, "I did read somewhere about a silver and something battery. It was strong as hell, but, of course, it's too expensive to be practical."

Captain Gringo smiled and said, "We don't have to be practical. We have to listen in on that damned cruiser. Run down to the officer's mess. I noticed some silver trays in the cupboard and, of course, we can flatten out some spoons if the trays won't be enough."

Porter blinked in astonishment. Then he nodded and said, "I don't see why it wouldn't work. The battery plates

149

don't have to be neat. They just have to be more or less flat and hang near the copper in the acid!"

Porter left. Captain Gringo rolled a map out on the chart table and tried to find the river they were anchored in. He couldn't. It wasn't on the map. That was the best news he'd had all morning.

Gaston came in. The dapper little Frenchman said, "Ah, there you are. I didn't see you at breakfast. Hung over?"

"Sort of. I washed a mess of Moors and Christians down with more booze than I should of and it's all just sitting there."

"You have my sympathy. Staying aboard *Thistlegorm* all night occasioned some comment."

"I noticed. Before you say it, I just knocked Malo on his ass for asking how I liked rosy-cheeked boys."

Gaston laughed and said, "Well, MacTavish is inclined to walk *tres* delicately, but if I know you, some Indian wench is still twitching. I don't suppose it occurred to you that your old friend, Gaston, has been lonely?"

Captain Gringo laughed and said, "As a matter of fact, I think I can fix you up, tonight. But let's worry about getting through the day."

He filled Gaston in on his adventures aboard *Thistlegorm* and since getting back aboard *La Tortuga,* leaving out some of the dirty parts.

Gaston nodded sagely when he was through and said, *"Eh bien,* it is time to reconsider our options. We'd better, how you say, ditch this gang of guerrillas and deserters, Dick."

"I don't see how we can do that, Gaston."

"You don't? *Merde,* we only started out to rescue Porter. These others would not be our responsibility, even if they weren't more ungrateful than the last batch we helped."

"I know they're a pretty useless bunch, with a few exceptions."

"Very well, let us take the exceptions and get out of here. Young MacTavish is not a fugitive. *Thistlegorm* has ship's papers. If we took off with him and went to this Uruba place until the heat died down . . ."

"It's more complicated than that. In the first place, I think the others may be making similar plans. I just tried to explain the errors of his ways to Gomez. I'm not sure I succeeded."

Porter came back, grinning, with a stack of trays piled high with silverware. Gaston raised a curious eyebrow, but asked Captain Gringo, "Do you suppose Gomez is the troublemaker we've been worried about?"

Captain Gringo said, "It's starting to look that way. He was sort of useless in the old Balboa Brigade and he sucks around too much for a guy with a clear conscience. I guess he thinks, as a vet, he rates a bit more rank in this new outfit."

Porter put down the silver and said, "I missed something. Who's double-crossing whom, *now?* I swear to God, nobody back home would *believe* the back-stabbing and wheels within wheels down here in Banana Land!"

He took a pair of pliers from his hip pocket and began to flatten out a spoon as Gaston asked, "New hobby?"

Captain Gringo explained, "We need new battery plates. Bill thinks silver will do as well as zinc. Let's get back to MacTavish. He got a little coy with me, last night, when I asked about his home port. It seems to be a family secret."

"*Merde alors,* you mean he's a pirate, too, in addition to his other vices?"

"We didn't get into his other vices. He's not an outlaw. I guess he has some sort of forged papers for *Thistlegorm,* since he bought her fair and square on the open market. His folks are left-over Scots who never saw fit to take out citizenship papers with any government, once Scotland lost interest in them. They have a good thing going for them. They have some jungle settlement nobody knows about. They fish and pearl for such ready cash as they might need. No rent. No taxes. No problems with the outside world. They seem to be living under the old clan system. MacTavish says his old man is a chief. That accounts for Mac being sent to Kiel to buy the new schooner."

Gaston said, "Being the chief's son would account for

nobody laughing too much about his *other* habits, too. Did he outright refuse to tell you where this Celtic utopia might be?"

"Sort of. Every time I tried to pin him down, he batted his eyelashes at me. We both got pretty drunk and everything was sort of up in the air when we went to bed."

Porter looked up, startled, and Captain Gringo growled, "He went to bed alone and I spent the night with a couple of pearl divers. *Female* pearl divers."

Porter said, "Oh," and went back to work, looking relieved.

Gaston chuckled and said, *"Eh bien,* I see we have to be *practique.* We obviously can't stay here forever. Somehow, we must get on the good side of young Mac-Tavish."

Captain Gringo said, "Forget it. I'm not sure which of his sides he considers the best one, but count me out."

Porter said, "Don't look at me. I'm a married man."

Gaston said, "Ah, but that would give you a certain detachment, *non?* I suggested we approach the problem in a detached *practique* manner. Nobody has to fall in love with the imbecile. It would suffice if we could get Mac-Tavish to feel more friendly to one of us."

Porter grimaced. Captain Gringo said, "It's your idea, Gaston. Why don't you go over and give the poor kid a break?"

Gaston shrugged and said, "I have this ridiculous problem. I told you the old Legion took a *practique* view of sex when there were no women to be, uh, drafted."

"All the more reason for you to make the sacrifice, Gaston. I'd either laugh like hell or wind up hitting somebody at the last moment."

Gaston sighed and said, "I know. I remember, one time, when I was younger that either of you and *tres* passionate. I had not had a woman in months and there was this most effeminate Armenian lad in our old outfit. To make a long story short, one gets most fatigued making love to one's fist and, as time passed, and he kept making passes . . ."

Porter made a face and cut in, "Jesus, what was it

like? Did he take it in the bung or was he one of those crazy ones who like to suck?"

Gaston said, "I never found out. I had made up my mind, most firmly, that the next time he offered, I would take him up on it. But then, one night when we were alone, he kissed me."

"Yuch! I'll bet you hit him, right?"

"Mais non, that would have been cruel. As it was, I think I upset him terribly. You see, I laughed. I could not stop. He kissed quite nicely, to my surprise, and I tried to go along with it. But every time he reached for me, it tickled and I doubled up with laughter. In the end he flounced away, quite angry, and he never spoke to me again until, a few months later, the Tuareg got him, on patrol."

Porter said, "That's it? You sure tell pointless stories, Gaston."

Gaston said, "I know. A writer would give it a neater ending. But I only confessed to make my point. I do not think MacTavish would find me attractive, since I am the same size and a bit gray around the edges. But, even if he did, I could not have an affair with him. Worse yet, I would doubtless offend him and we'd lose any chance we had to obtain his help."

Porter said, "We could *force* him to show us the way to his hideout, couldn't we?"

The two soldiers of fortune exchanged glances. Captain Gringo said, "We're looking for another hideout, not another war. MacTavish doesn't live *alone* in Port Uruba. I'd rather fight the Colombian Army than a clan of pissed-off Highlanders on their own ground."

Gaston said, *"Oui.* It is up to you to find some way to get on better terms with MacTavish, then."

"I guess so. But there has to be a better way than what you have in mind, you dirty old goat."

20

For such a long lazy day, it felt tense as hell. There was nothing to do on either vessel but wait. The Indian girls couldn't even dive for pearls, this far up the little river. The water was too fresh for oysters. Gaston put the somewhat sullen engine room gang to work flushing *La Tortuga*'s boilers some more. They insisted the tubes were as clear as they were ever going to get, this side of a shipyard. And they were probably right, but it kept them out of mischief.

Those with no other duties lolled on the deck or plotted in odd corners. Malo had vanished somewhere to nurse his swollen face, which wouldn't have been much to worry about if they could be sure he sulked alone. But Gomez had vanished, too. They could have found him if they'd really looked, but they didn't bother. The oily Gomez would have a perfectly good excuse, since he wasn't *doing* anything, right?

Porter worked on the wireless set, with the doors all locked and a prudent pistol near at hand. By noon it was too hot to think, let alone stage a mutiny, so Captain Gringo went to his quarters to grab some siesta shut-eye. The river water cooled the plates and it wasn't as hot and stuffy below decks as it was topside.

He'd just gotten undressed when there was a discreet tap on the cabin door. He picked up his .38 and opened it a crack. A crack was all Cielita needed. She shoved her way in and whispered, "Angelo is up in the chain locker. They are having some sort of meeting."

That was interesting, so he didn't throw her out. As she noticed his nudity in the dim light, she said, "Oh, you knew I was coming, eh?"

He said, "As a matter of fact, I was about to take a nap."

"Alone? It is not healthy to nap alone, *querido*."

Before he could answer, Cielita was stripping, herself. Cielita stripped fast. She'd probably had a lot of practice. He needed her like he needed a dose of Yellow Jack, but she was dumb and liked to talk. He wanted to hear about the mysterious meeting in the bows more than he really wanted to sleep. So he put down the .38 and took her in his arms, saying, "Welcome back."

She rubbed her tawny curves against him as they stood belly to belly by the bunk. She said, "Oh, this is fun. Can we try it standing up?"

"If you want to. What are the guys having a meeting about, honey?"

Cielita reached down to fumble his shaft into place as she said, "I don't know. Angelo never tells me anything. He says I am his *mujer,* but he treats me as if I had no brains. That is what I like about you, Deek. You do not just stick it in and out. You talk to a woman like she was a person."

He moved her against the bulkhead and lowered his hips as she stood on tiptoe, thighs parted, and added, "I like this, too, of course. What is the matter? Are you not comfortable? It feels a bit tired."

He got it part way in, but said, "I *am* a little tired. It's sort of hot for acrobatics."

"Oh, let us move to the bed, then. I can't stay long. I would not take such a chance if you were not so nice. We must finish quickly."

She had no way of knowing how good that made him feel as he smiled and led her over to the bunk. He braced a pillow under her hips, aware he wasn't up to his usual standards, and as he started to mount her, Cielita warned, "Be careful, I feel very vulnerable in this position and there is so much of you, my all."

Actually, it worked out just right with the pillow. He was half limp when they started, but he'd forgotten how nicely she moved and he tried to please her. He didn't really care if he made it over the top himself, right now. Cielita was pretty and a good lay, **but** her stupidity and general availablity tended to dampen his enthusiasm. He realized he was just giving himself. It wasn't unpleasant. It just felt sort of dumb. He wondered if whores felt like this with a customer and decided they must. Her mounting excitement made him feel detached and a little superior. He reminded himself never to pay for it, if this was what it felt like at the other end. Meanwhile, as he laid her, he pumped her. Cielita was a nonstop talker, no matter what else she was doing, and so he dredged up a little more information as they made love. Angelo, as he'd guessed, was just a kid who'd do anything for anybody who kept telling him it was his idea. The treacherous Gomez was the problem. It wasn't clear whether Gomez had real plans or just liked to plot, as he sucked and fawned all over. The American knew he could get Gomez back on his own side just by letting him feel important. They could win him over by promoting him to Third Mate. Maybe if Porter had any silver left over, they could make a badge for Gomez to wear. That would probably do it. He'd bully the shit out of everyone, then, and that would end it, until some other asshole decided he was a Man of Destiny.

Cielita said she was coming. So he helped her get there while he tried to decide if joining her was worth the effort. The advantage of a lukewarm passion was that he could probably keep this up for hours, if there'd been any point to it.

Cielita went limp and began to coo and caress his back and buttocks, so he just relaxed and lay still, soaking. That was the position they were in when the door popped open and a female voice gasped, "Oh!"

It was Cathy. Captain Gringo looked up and sighed, "Sorry. I was sure the door was locked."

Cathy said, "Oh," some more, and shut the door with an angry slam as she lit out for parts unknown. Cielita opened her eyes and asked, "What happened? I heard a noise, but I was up in heaven, just now."

He said, "It's not important. You'd better get out of here, though."

"Can we do it some more, later?"

156

"Maybe. But, next time, wait for an invitation. These popping doors are starting to get on my nerves."

Cielita rose as he rolled off. She dressed as quickly as she'd stripped. He watched, bemused, and wondered if she was putting out to anyone else aboard. It wouldn't have surprised him much to learn she had been. It was sort of comforting to know Angelo was too arrogant to notice.

After she left he swabbed himself down with a damp rag and sat on the bunk to have a smoke in the nude.

There was another rap on the door and again the damned thing popped open. Cathy stepped in, still clad in that open kimono, and seemed braced for an argument until she saw he was alone. Cathy said, "Oh, you got rid of her, eh?"

He said, "There's something wrong with that door. I keep locking the son of a bitch and you keep opening it."

"Deek, I had to talk to you. I realize I was unfair to both of us."

He stood up, went to the door, and opened it as Cathy sat on the bunk. He saw there was a latch button built into the edge and said, "Oh, I get it. You have to push this doodad to make it stay locked."

He made sure, this time. As he turned from the door, Cathy had her kimono off. She was on the same pillow in a come-and-get-it position. The contrast of her paler skin and thinner build was stimulating. But he said, "I thought we'd agreed it was over, Cathy."

She said, "I know. That is what drove you into the arms of that silly little *mestiza* slut, no?"

"I guess so. I thought you'd left mad."

"Oh, I was most shocked and very angry when I caught you, just now. But then I realized why you'd done it, poor baby. I let you down to suddenly. I know what you men are like when you feel deprived."

He really didn't think he ought to laugh at a lady in that position. So he didn't. But it wasn't easy. Cathy giggled roguishly as she stared at his body in the semi-darkness. She said, "I see no other woman can really satisfy you, after all. You are a dreadfully passionate man, my *toro*. I only came back for to tell you I forgave you, and for to suggest a discreet meeting later on, tonight, after you'd had time to recover. But when I dashed in to face that enormous erection . . . ah, why talk about it. Let us *do* it, no?"

So they did it. And this time he had no trouble at all. He'd about recovered from the orgy aboard *Thistlegorm,* and the almost pointless quicky with Cielita had recharged his batteries. Cathy was the prettiest thing aboard either vessel and her pale flesh was a nice novelty. He tried to compare her body with XiXi's dark and different desirability. It aroused him further. But some part of his brain remained oddly detached. It wasn't that he'd been getting too much. The sex part was fine. But nobody *meant* anything to anybody. He knew women bitched and wailed about just being used. He'd used a lot of them in his time. But he hadn't had a woman since poor little Luisa, back on that steamer, that he'd felt like knowing, above the waist.

The Indian girls were cute little animals who'd have taken care of him if he'd had two heads. Cielita was a little pig and Cathy, while bright and pretty, had her head screwed on funny. She kept changing her mind too fast for him to follow, and her husband was supposed to be dangerous, too.

But, what the hell, it was siesta time and he had nothing better to do. She was awfully nice on the sheets and he might as well enjoy it while it lasted. She could enter a convent any minute, the way she dithered on about what was best for everyone. He wondered if she was just killing a siesta, too. When you got right down to it, a body was a body, right?

Cathy broke into his train of thought by sighing, "That was lovely. Let me up. I want to try something new."

He got off and she swung her legs off the bed to bend and reach for her kimono on the floor. She presented an interesting view, bent over like that. Her pale rump stimulated him to new naughty thoughts. It was an angle he hadn't tried, with Cathy.

She sat up again, pivoting on one naked hip, and few men in his position would have had a chance. But he saw the flash of steel in her upraised hand and was moving even before she blurted, "He who betrays me *dies,* you *Yanqui* bastard!"

158

He caught her wrist as the knife arched down at his naked gut. She glared wildly and tried to rake his face with the nails of her free hand as he struggled to control her without hurting her. He saw he couldn't. So he shrugged and hung a right cross on her jaw.

He didn't hit her hard—just hard enough to stun her. The knife dropped on his belly, fortunately handle first, and he brushed it off to the floor as he hauled her across his hips, sat up, and gave her a good spanking.

Cathy moaned but refused to scream as he paddled her pale derriere a nice shade of dusky rose. He stopped when he heard her sobbing instead of cursing. He rested his stinging palm on her stung buttocks and said, "I'll let you up, if you'll promise to behave."

"You big bully. I'll kill you for this."

"You already tried. I've been meaning to ask you about that. Did you have any reason for waving that knife at me just now or is it just that time of the month?"

"You betrayed me with another woman, you animal!"

"Oh, I get it. You're a pretty cold-blooded cunt, Cathy. That faked orgasm was just to set me up for revenge, huh?"

She struggled to raise her belly from his lap. But he held her in place and said, "Steady, girl. We'll just sort this out a bit before I turn you loose."

She pounded the mattress with her fist and said, "I hate you, I hate you, I hate you! You had no right to make love to another woman after I gave myself to you!"

He pet her absently as he said, "Aw, shit, Cathy. You just got through telling me you had a husband and that we were through. Who says you're the only one good enough to play musical beds?"

"Its not the same. I *saw* you making love to that other woman, right before my very eyes!"

"Sure, and if your husband opened the door right now he'd see you bare-assed with another man. You can't have things both ways, honey. If you can do it, I can do it. It's a game any number can play."

She said, "Take your fingers out of there, you brute. I am sorry I ever met you. I wish for to be with my Benito. I never want for you to touch me again."

He moved his hand further in between her trembling

buttocks and said, "Sorry. You've gotten me sort of excited as well as pissed off. I think I'll just tear off a piece while I figure out some safe way to let go of you."

She protested, "Stop that! I don't want to. You wouldn't rape me, would you, Deek?"

"Why not? You just tried to kill me."

He rolled her off his lap and shoved her across the bed, checking quickly for the knife and spotting it in a safe far corner. Cathy rolled on her stomach and said, "I won't turn over for you."

He shrugged, got a grip on her hip bones from either side, and lifted as he knelt on the edge of the mattress. She was already well lubricated albeit unprepared for his move, and before she grasped his intent, he was in her. She gasped. "Oh, no, you're in the wrong place!"

He said, "What's the difference? You said you didn't like it anywhere."

So she sobbed and beat the mattress with both fists as he abused her rather brutally from the rear. He knew he'd feel like a shit doing this to any *nice* girl. But sex mingled nicely with revenge and he couldn't bring himself to really give her the beating she had coming, from her husband as well as himself.

It was an odd thrill to mistreat the sobbing little would-be murderess this way. He could see why some guys did it more often. He knew he'd never get another chance like this, since he tried to avoid troubled women. So he let himself go, to see if he'd been missing anything.

He enjoyed sodomy-rape more than he'd expected to. The idea had never appealed to him before, so it was all brand new. He got a thrill from the sight of her abused pale rump as he pounded her. He withdrew, rolled her over, and lowered himself brutally but more normally on her panting curvacious torso. As he entered her frontally, she sobbed, "Oh, thank you! That other way was killing me."

She wrapped her arms and legs around him and started moving to meet his desire. He laughed and said, "I thought you hated me, Cathy."

"Oh, I do. I've never hated a man so much in my life. But, *Madre de Dios,* you fuck so good!"

160

21

The last time he saw Cathy she was thoroughly confused as well as abused. She made him promise, again, not to tell anybody she'd been cheating on General Puma. He'd agreed, of course. With any luck, she wouldn't try to knife him again until she could get him alone with a knife. She was great in bed, but a little fatiguing.

He went to the radio shack and asked Porter how the silverware idea had worked. Porter was seated at the table, taking something down. He stopped and said, "They just signed off. The new battery plates are fantastic! A guy could make a fortune if he could put a silver battery on the market!"

"If he had that much silver he wouldn't need a fortune. He'd already have one. What did you just pick up, Bill?"

"It wasn't the cruiser. The Colombian government sent it to them, I guess. It's in Spanish. I took it down, but I have to study it before I can make out what it says in English."

Capain Gringo picked up the pad and said, "You *write* lousy Spanish, too. From now on, take it down phonetically, letter by letter."

He read the untidy scrawl and added, "Shit. It's an all-points bulletin. Fighting has broken out on the mainland. Colombia just won the first round. They advise everyone to be on the lookout for General Puma. He seems to be headed this way with what's left of his army."

"Oh, great. He's on the same side as our own rebels, right?"

"Who knows? There's more. There's a column of Colombian infantry hot on General Puma's heels. Bogota is asking everyone to hold their fire until they make sure of any targets on shore. Both the forces have irregulars in peasant dress along. So we have two ragged-ass bands with guns playing tag in that green hell out around us. They're not in contact. So it's an even-money bet who makes it this far first."

The wireless started clicking and Porter said, "Hold it. This one's in English."

He wrote in block letters as he listened to the Morse in his earphones. When he'd finished, he handed it up to Captain Gringo. The message was from "Fleet" and read, "FLAG TO *H.M.S. DUNRAVEN.* WHAT IS GOING ON? DO YOU EVER INTEND TO REJOIN US, OR HAVE YOU DECIDED TO GO NATIVE? PLEASE REPORT WHEN YOU EXPECT TO RESUME YOUR PATROL ON STATION!"

Porter said, "It looks like they're up to something sneaky, Dick. They haven't moved all day and they don't seem to have any explanations to offer. Do you think they've spotted us?"

"We'd be ducking sixteen-inchers right now if they knew for sure where to send them. I don't know what they're up to, either. Stay with it."

He went out to the wheelhouse. Gaston had just climbed up from the engine room. Gaston said, "I think the engines would get us as far as the Gulf of Darien, now. When do you intend to seduce MacTavish?"

Captain Gringo glanced over at the schooner, sitting just a pistol shot away on the mirror-slick water. He said, "I'll *talk* to him. I'll leave his fair white body to you, you old fart."

Gaston cackled and recited, "There was an old man named Bruno. He said, about screwing I do know. A dog is just fine, and a woman's divine, but a young boy is *numero uno!*"

"That's not funny, Gaston. I said I'd try to talk him into giving away some family secrets. He seems like a nice little guy and I don't think he expects any favors like that. But I'll feel better talking to MacTavish if you'll get off the subject long enough for me to forget he's sort of elfin."

Porter came out with another sheet of paper. He said, "The cruiser says they've anchored to scrape barnacles. Does that make any sense to either of you?"

Captain Gringo said, "No, but they probably couldn't come up with anything better. They must not have a prearranged code, but the cruiser skipper has found out we have a Marconi set and he's being cute."

Porter nodded and said, "I'm sort of tempted to tap out a message to them. If I said we were a merchant freighter and that we'd just seen a gunboat headed somewhere else . . ."

"Don't you dare!" Captain Gringo cut in, adding, "Didn't you know a foxy radio man can home in on a signal with his antenna?"

"I do now," said Porter, abashed.

Gaston said, "Getting them to chase us somewhere else sounds like a fine idea, Bill. Dick's smoke signals fooled them once. But we could hardly put a Marconi set in a lifeboat and cast it adrift."

Gaston spotted the thoughtful look in Captain Gringo's eyes and, knowing him better than Porter, added, "Could we, Dick?"

Captain Gringo said, "No. Not a lifeboat. Somebody has to send the signal, give them time to take a bearing on it, and move out pronto, ahead of the first ranging shells."

He stared out the side window at the nearby *Thistlegorm* and said, "It'd be a lot of work. But if we hauled all this radio crap aboard that schooner and waited until dark, I see an outside chance. *Thistlegorm* can run rings around that schooner or any steam vessel. If we run well out to sea, sent a pirate message of some kind in the clear, and then moved back here out of sight . . ."

Gaston cut in with, "MacTavish would be risking his schooner as well as his tight little ass. Do you think you can talk him into it, Dick?"

"I guess I'll have to."

"Ooh, la! la! Who shall bend over for whom, you naughty boy?"

Before Captain Gringo could answer, Gomez came into the wheelhouse alone. Gomez had his hat in hand, but was wearing a rather smug expression as he announced, "I have just returned from a patrol with good news, Señores. Malo is making the gun turrets ready and Angelo says he can have the steam up any time we need it."

Captain Gringo frowned and said, "Back up. What do you mean about a patrol? I ordered no patrol."

Gomez grinned and said, "I meant no disrespect, Señor. I would have told you of our plans, but you were entertaining General Puma's woman in your cabin."

So there it was, like a spit in the face. They were down to "Señor" from "my Captain," eh? Gomez continued, "As I was saying, I felt you did not wish for to be disturbed. So I took some *muchachos* in the launch and we felt our way through the coastal swamps for to see if there was another way out to sea, besides this river's mouth."

"So, what did you find out?"

"There is no channel deep enough for *La Tortuga*'s keel, alas. But I bring good news. That British cruiser is a few kilometers up the coast. Dead in the water."

"That's good news?"

"*Si,* she seems to have run aground. Malo is a sailor. He knows about such things. Her waterline is too high for her to be afloat. The tide was out and he says she has to be resting on the bottom."

Captain Gringo thought before he nodded and said, "That makes sense, even considering the source. I assume you haven't mentioned anything you saw through my keyhole to anyone?"

Gomez grinned and said, "No. Not yet. *Los muchachos* are simple *peons*. They might not understand us men of the world. I, ah, did take the liberty of telling them you had made me your second in command. Was I wrong, Señor?"

"No. I've misjudged you, Gomez. You've been doing your homework since you were a private in the old Balboa Brigade."

"Es verdad. One grows weary of the taking of orders. But, now that we understand one another, this is my plan. We shall dart out of here while the tide is low and that cruiser is still stuck in the mud, eh?"

Gaston's lips paled and he put a hand on his pistol grips. But Captain Gringo shot him a warning look and managed a light tone as he asked Gomez, "Didn't you say you wanted *second* in command, *compañero?*"

Gomez shrugged and said, "I am content to leave the details of running the ship to you. I am a modest man who is willing to delegate authority and there has been some discussion about my seamanship. Malo says he should be captain, since he was, after all, a sailor. I spoke up in your behalf, since I am your friend. All in all, it will be best not to have any sudden changes in command, eh?"

"Yeah, mutiny can get to be a habit, once everyone sees how easy it is. But since you seem to be so big-hearted about details, your idea stinks. If we fire the boilers they'll spot our smoke. You did say they're just a few miles away, right?"

"*Si,* but stuck in the mud."

"Screw the mud. Those sixteen-inch guns can fire a shell over the horizon."

He saw the deflated look in the sneak's eyes and took a few inches back by saying, "If we move at all, it will have to be after dark."

"That is what I meant." Said Gomez.

"Yeah. There's more. Just getting out of this river puts us right back in the wrong end of the bowling alley. *La Tortuga* is slow as her namesake and the whole damned world seems to be looking for her. Before we make a run from this safe hideout, we'd better figure out where the hell we're running. Just before you came in to bring us all the good news we were doping out a few ideas about the subject."

Gomez nodded and said, "I told you I would leave the details to you. I am content to deal with larger things. This gunboat can be most useful to *La Revolucion.* As I see my mission, it is simply to get *La Tortuga* to safety and contact General Puma . . . about having this armored ship at my disposal, of course. I see no need to concern myself in family matters."

Nobody argued. So Gomez struck a Nelsonian pose and asked, "What are these plans of yours?"

Gaston blinked in surprise and even the inexperienced Porter seemed confused when Captain Gringo said, truthfully, "We were talking about moving this radio equipment over to the schooner. While you guys get *La Tortuga* ready for a sea run, we'll send *Thistlegorm* out in the wrong direction, sending dots and dashes all over the airways. The cruiser will range on the beam and, meanwhile, *La Tortuga* can slip out quietly and make her escape."

Gomez didn't understand. So Captain Gringo had to explain radio ranging a couple of times before the would-be admiral shrugged and said, "It is worth a try. I agree to your plan, save for one, ah, small detail."

"What's that, *amigo?*"

"Your friends may take this mysterious electrical gear over there and play with it. I need you here, in case I need your further assistance."

It wasn't very subtle. But what the hell, Captain Gringo had been a hostage before, and he knew Gaston could give the oily Gomez lessons in Machiavellian fun and games. So he smiled pleasantly and said, "Sure. No problem. They won't need me over there."

He smiled at Gaston and said, "You understand the plan, don't you? You and Porter get the Marconi stuff over to *Thistlegorm* and explain to MacTavish. Uh, make sure he understands that he's not to move out before we signal him to. That diesel can start up at a moment's notice but *La Tortuga* needs time to bring her boilers to full pressure."

Gaston nodded and said, "But of course. We will not wish to leave before dark in any case. I will wave my hat to you when we are all set and you will of course signal us when your friends are set to start the charade."

"Right. Let's detail a work crew and start loading this shit in the launch. With your permission, of course, Señor Gomez?"

Gomez nodded, but said, "I think I would like for

to be called 'Captain,' too. I mean no disrespect, but there is room for two captains aboard such a big vessel, no?"

"I guess so. To save your crew the confusion of sorting us out, why don't you call yourself the ship's master?"

"Master Gomez? I like it. What kind of a hat does a ship's master wear?"

Captain Gringo was tempted to suggest a dunce cap, but he didn't say so. He turned to Porter and said, "Stick with Gaston and do as he says and you'll be all right, Bill."

Porter said, "I hope so. The scenery sure shifts a lot down here. If I ever write that book I told you about it will have to be a farce."

22

Only a few hours had passed and the sun was still above the treetops, but it had seemed a million years since Gaston and Porter had rowed over to the schooner with the radio gear.

Captain Gringo stood on the bridge wing, leaning an elbow on the breech of the Maxim mounted out there. Inside, Gomez was talking to Catalina Lopez O'Hara y Batista, who'd also gotten sort of important all of a sudden. He couldn't hear what they were arguing about, but he assumed it was either about him or who was in charge these days. It just made him feel weary. The main reason he enjoyed a reputation as a leader, down here, was that most people who hired him were tired of the endless bickering about command. Every rebel who could read a newspaper considered him- or herself a general.

To be fair, many of the mercurial people south of Laredo were bright as well as sometimes insanely brave. War was an art of elephantine simplicity, once you'd memorized a few basic rules, and one plan was as good as another, a lot of times. But the thing that bogged down so many revolutions was an inborn inability to make one plan and stick with it. No army or navy can function as a debating society. You have to pick out one leader and follow him, even when you wonder what the hell he thinks he's doing.

Latin American military units reminded him of the Ancient Greeks. They'd been good fighting men in their day, and from the Trojan Horse to Marathon they'd shown they could fight trickily as well as bravely.

What had done them in was their habit of debating every move before a battle. The Romans hadn't been braver, tougher, or smarter. They'd just cleaned up on the Greeks and everybody else by simple soldiering. Some of the Roman generals had been assholes who'd make George Armstrong Custer look brilliant. No Greek hoplite, or Hispanic guerrilla, would have followed Varus into that German forest or Custer into Little Big Horn. They were too smart and too independent to be good soldiers. So the dumb unimaginative Romans had simply marched over them in a mess of set-piece battles. The poor Greeks had never understood how such clods had beaten them. The guys down here couldn't see how their pisspot dictators did it, either. And it seemed a waste of time to try and tell them.

Over on *Thistlegorm*, one of the Indian girls was lashing a reefed sail. Gaston came out to the cockpit and moved casually to the mounted Gatling gun before he took off his hat and waved it. Captain Gringo waved back. He didn't know how Gaston had done it. Maybe he hadn't laughed, this time, when a fairy kissed him, or maybe MacTavish was just sensible. At any rate, they were all set over there and the timing was just right.

Captain Gringo glanced around, got a good grip on the machine gun, and lifted it from its mount. As he moved toward the end of the wing with it, Gomez came out of the wheelhouse and gasped, "What are you doing with that gun, Señor?"

The tall American smiled wolfishly and said, "I was about to throw it overboard, but what the hell, as long as you're here . . ."

Gomez went for his sidearm as Captain Gringo swung the muzzle of the cocked and primed Maxim his way and fired. The short savage burst blew Gomez in half at the waist and sent bits and pieces of him into the wheelhouse as Cathy screamed and, unfortunately, dove for cover.

A bullet spanged off the wing rail near Captain Gringo and he swung the heavy weapon to cover the foredeck. He spotted the man who'd fired at him, peering around the foreward gun turret, gun in hand. So he fired another burst and chipped paint and brains away as, slowly, the gun turret started to turn.

He hadn't thought of that. The architects of *La Tortuga* hadn't thought, when they gave those turrets a 360-degree capacity, that anyone would ever be asshole enough to aim at their own conning tower. But Malo was an asshole for sure. He obviously wasn't thinking about the future as he tried to train his four-inchers at his own wheelhouse.

Captain Gringo braced the Maxim on the rail and fired into the gun turret's narrow-aiming slit. He couldn't tell how many rounds wound up inside the turret, but some did, because he heard them bouncing around inside, above the sound of screaming.

Not waiting to see whether the turret was still moving, he tossed the machine gun overboard, took a deep breath, and followed it in a long two-story dive.

His plunge took him deep enough to brush the soft bottom with his outstretched fingers and he started swimming hard, underwater, for *Thistlegorm*. He stayed as deep as he could for as long as he could and the water around him throbbed to the muffled rumble of the diesel engine in *Thistlegorm*'s steel hull. He wasn't sure how far he had to go, but he had to breathe, damn it, so he surfaced, gulped air, and ducked under again as a bullet spanged into the water over him. The next time he came up for a gulp of air he heard the woodpecker chatter of the Gatling gun, and no bullets landed near him. Gaston was sweeping *La Tortuga* with drum fire to discourage sniping. Hooray for Gaston.

The American in the water was a little out of shape from the only exercise he'd been getting lately and his wet clothes and boots were a bitch to swim in. He unbuckled his gunbelt and let it go. It helped a little, but he'd never make it in these fucking boots.

Then hands grabbed him on either side and in the murky underwater light he could see XiXi and Xoxocatl had him by the arms. He didn't think they'd swum all this way to screw him, and as he saw the keel of *Thistlegorm* ahead he knew they hadn't. He tried to surface, but they resisted and kept swimming as the keel passed over the three of them. He caught on and thought, "Right. Come up under the cover of the far side, if we don't drown in the process."

They made it. But he'd never tasted air as good as that first deep gasp when they surfaced at last. The Indian girls were laughing and one of them tweeked his crotch as other hands reached down to haul him aboard.

Thistlegorm was starting to move, already, as he rose from the tingling deck and MacTavish warned, "Keep your head doon. We're twa inches taller than me cabin!"

He bent slightly as he saw it had been Mac and another Indian girl who'd hauled him bodily aboard. XiXi and Xoxocatl slid over the low rail like a pair of sexy brown sea lions. So they were all set and why the hell was MacTavish still hanging on to him?

MacTavish stared up into his face and said, "Och, Dick, I feared we'd lost ye!"

Then MacTavish kissed him, full on the lips, and said something stupid like "Darling."

The startled American instinctively put a gentle hand on Mac's chest to shove him away, saying, "Hey, come on, Mac."

Then his eyes widened, and when MacTavish tried to kiss him again, he let her. Old Mac was a little flat-chested, but old Mac was not a guy. No guy had tits of any size, and she wasn't bad looking, either, once you realized that short red hair went with a female body.

Mac moved his hands away from her firm little breast as she said, "Och, my lassies are watching. This is nae the time to lose our wee heads. I have to take the wheel."

She turned and moved aft to the cockpit as he followed, staring at her rear view with new respect. It was no wonder she'd made him so uncomfortable. He'd never been attracted to a homosexual before and his instincts had messed his head up. He didn't have to ask Mac why she wore male sailing attire. Along with her short hair, it had probably saved her from rape when the pirates boarded her vessel. But, Jesus, she might have *told* a guy before she started batting her eyes at him like that!

They joined Gaston in the cockpit. Another naked Indian lady was at the helm and they were moving down the river nicely as the little Frenchman bounced Gatling rounds off *La Tortuga*. Gaston glanced over his shoulder and said, *"Merde,* you certainly took your time. It is almost sunset."

Captain Gringo said, "You're wasting ammo, damn it. Can't you see we're almost out of range? As for my timing, I think I timed it neat as hell. Mac, here, has papers if we're stopped at sea. Those clowns can't put out to sea before dark unless they want to have their smoke plume spotted."

Porter came out of the cabin. He said, "There's not a thing on the air. Won't somebody tell me what in hell is going on? First we're busting our humps to save that gunboat and now we're running away from her. I'm confused as hell, guys."

MacTavish said, "Och, ye say ye're confused? I know less than ye do, and I was raised doon here."

She took the wheel from the Indian girl and said something to her in Carib. The girl left and Mac asked, "Does anyone here have any idea where we're bound?"

Captain Gringo said, "Can't you take us to Uruba, Mac?"

The red-head frowned and said, "I dinna ken. I'm nae supposed to bring unexpected guests to supper. We'll hae to study on that alang the way. But, och, it's obvious ye canna stay *here!"*

As if to punctuate her remark, a cotton ball of gun-smoke materialized from *La Tortuga*'s gun turret and a four-inch shell skipped over the water like a stone to explode with a roar of a pistol shot to starboard.

Gaston spat and said, *"Merde.* Whoever is manning that turret is a terrible shot. Who did you leave in charge, Dick?"

Captain Gringo said, "It's either Cathy or Malo. They're both mad at me. You'll be pleased to know I knocked off Gomez as I was leaving."

La Tortuga fired again. The shell hit closer. Gaston said, *"Eh bien,* but I am not *that* pleased. *Regardez!* They are starting the engines! See the smoke from the funnel?"

172

"Oh boy. They really are mad, aren't they. Can we go any faster, Mac?"

"Nae, but yon gunboat won't be up to full steam for a few minutes and she'll nae be able to match our speed when she is. I could loft our sails, once we're oot to sea. That would give us a few more knots."

"It could screw up our ability to maneuver, too. It's safer to just run on the engine for now."

"Ay, we do agree on some things after all. We're almost to the river's mouth. Which way do ye suggest?"

Gaston gasped, "Which way? *Merde alors,* there is a British cruiser to port. Which way *can* we go but starboard?"

Captain Gringo said, "Port it is, Mac. Make a beeline for that cruiser. Porter, get back on the wireless. If that grounded cruiser signals as we pass her, tell her we're being chased by a gunboat and haven't time to stay and chat."

"What if they order us to heave to, Dick?"

"I'm hoping they won't. But if they do, we'll have no choice. There's a fifty-fifty chance we can bluff them. They're not looking for this schooner and they'll just see four whites and some Indians. Not the Hispanic rebels they're after."

Porter grimaced and said, "I wish you hadn't said fifty-fifty, Dick."

"Hey, Bill, what do you want, egg in your beer? Fifty-fifty are *good* odds, down here!"

Mac said, "We're almost there. I can see the open sea beyond yon bar."

Captain Gringo nodded and told Gaston, "Find a tarp and cover that Gatling. It might make the Royal Navy curious or even nervous."

Gaston said, "I wish we still had the Maxim. We could use all the guns we could get. Even if we bluff past the cruiser these are not friendly waters."

The girl Mac had sent below came back with drinks on a tray as Gaston was covering the Gatling. Mac raised her glass to Captain Gringo's and said, "To us, Dick. I know ye prefer more meat on women, but to friendship, anyway."

He wasn't sure how to take that, but this was hardly the time to sort out their relationship. As they headed up the Mosquito Coast he thought back to the events in Mac's cabin. Hadn't she figured out why he'd spurned her coy advances by now? Hell, she must know he'd taken her for a guy. It had been her idea to dress like one. If she'd only told him . . . But she must have assumed he'd known. You *could* see she was a lean and boyish but definite female, once you looked close. He could tell her, he supposed, but how was a lady going to take that? She was still peeved at him for passing her up for XiXi and Xoxocatl. She'd really be pissed if he told her she looked so sexless to him that he'd taken her for a boy!

He sipped his glass of gin and tonic and said, "I've been meaning to ask you, Mac. Don't you have a first name?"

She said, "It's Flora. But I'm used to Mac. Everyone has always called me that, for some reason. Mac will do me nicely, thank ye."

"Mac it is," he grinned.

Gaston, staring aft, said, *"Regardez!* That smoke plume from *La Tortuga* is moving! The idiots are following us!"

Captain Gringo turned, stared soberly, and said, "Relax. They can't be dumb enough to be following us. They're probably going to swing away at the river mouth. They should have waited until dark like I told them. But we'd noticed they weren't too keen on taking orders from a gringo."

Overhead, the sunset sky was zipped open by what sounded like a garbage can rolling over railroad ties, and as the dull boom of the cruiser's gun was echoed by a louder explosion near *La Tortuga*'s smoke, he added, "See what I mean?"

Mac swung the wheel hard over and said, "Och, we're right in the middle of it all!"

Captain Gringo shoved her away from the wheel, swung it back the other way, and said, "Steady as she goes. They're not firing at us. They're ranging on that smoke plume. They don't even know we're here."

And then *H.M.S. Dunraven* made a liar out of him

by rounding the next bend with a bone in her teeth, sixteen-inch guns blazing and her white battle ensign flying!

Captain Gringo muttered, "Jee-zuss!" and swung the helm shoreward to get out of the way as he added, "I see they rode the rising tide off the mud after all."

Mac said, "Och, they mean to run us doon!"

But as *Thistlegorm* darted for the shallows like a minnow trying to avoid a big gray shark, the cruiser's guns fired again, and it was obvious they weren't the intended target. The smaller schooner shuddered to a stop as her keel dug into the offshore mud. But as they lay there, helpless, the cruiser tore past them at flank speed, as if they'd been invisible.

Captain Gringo reached for the engine controls by the wheel and reversed the screw as the waves of the cruiser's wake rolled in over the shallows. They backed off in a series of soft bumps and he said, "Thank you," with a wry grin.

Bill Porter came out with a puzzled frown on his face and a paper in his hand. He held it out and Captain Gringo took it. It read, "SCHOONER AHOY. SORRY. H.M.S. DUNRAVEN."

Captain Gringo nodded and said, "Better get back on the earphones, Bill. The next few minutes might be interesting."

He put the screw in forward gear, but at half speed as they moved on, hugging the flats. Mac asked him what he thought he was doing and he said, "Looking for a cove to shelter in. If they take anybody back there alive, they'll be back. And we can't outrun that cruiser *or* its guns!"

He spotted an inlet a mile up the coast and as they tooled slowly in, they could hear the distant sound of big guns. Gaston opined some of the explosions sounded like four-inchers and he said, "Yeah, poor bastards. I knew that Malo didn't have much sense."

"Would you have surrendered without firing back, Dick?"

"No. I don't have much sense, either. But I'm a better shot than Malo."

23

It was after dark and they lay in a shallow lagoon screened by mangroves when they spotted the cruiser again, moving majestically under her running lights like she owned the sea. She probably thought she did. Porter came out to join them on deck. He said, "They've stopped sending for the night. Jesus, to hear them tell it, they just won the Battle of Trafalgar."

"Any prisoners?" asked Captain Gringo, bleakly.

Porter said, "Apparently not. The Limeys say they blew *La Tortuga* out of the water after she resisted. They say they took a couple of four-inchers and one British seaman caught a shell fragment in the leg. They're taking him to the nearest British base."

"That'll be Bluefields. We're home free, kiddies. Everybody looking for us thinks we're dead."

Mac said, "We canna stay among these mangroves much longer. The mosquitos are already oot and it'll be worse in an hour. I'm for yon open main and a night sail away from these waters."

"Are you ready to take us to Uruba, Mac?"

He saw her hesitation and soothed, "Later. First things first. I don't think we should be out on the open sea when the sun comes up. That battle is going to attract a lot of attention and there's no telling how many navy types we might meet out there with no place to duck."

"Ay, but we have to be *somewhere* by sunrise, Dick."

"Okay. Let's put back to that river. The bugs aren't

bad, out over running water. There'll be nobody there, now, and I want to see if your divers can get that machine gun off the bottom for me."

"Och, we have a machine gun, Dick."

"I know. Two will be even better. Like I said, noise attracts a crowd and I stand corrected on piracy in these waters. Three men and a mess of damned tough women ought to be able to stand off anybody, with a machine gun fore and aft. It's only a short run. We'll shelter there until we know it's safe to start fishing or whatever again."

Mac shrugged and said, "Awheel, I'm in nae hurry, and there were some pearls in the estuary. I'll be in me cabin if ye need me."

She left and Gaston moved over to say, "I shall take the helm, my old and rare. Don't you know an invitation when you hear one?"

"For Chrissake, Gaston. Don't you ever think of anything else? She said she was going to her cabin. She didn't ask anyone to go along."

"*Merde alors,* she said she would be there if you needed her. Need her, you idiot. If not for the sake of your poor deprived genitals, think of it as a sacrifice for Bill and me. We have to stay on her good side, and, with a woman, that is always her inside."

He ducked inside and made his way to Mac's cabin, painfully aware of the one right across the companionway where he'd made noisy love to two of her crew. She'd probably kill him if he made a pass at her. But if he couldn't talk her into taking them to her colony, at least he might get her to put them ashore someplace they'd have a chance. If they could somehow make it back to the Costa Rican highlands, the local cops wouldn't be looking for them there. Costa Rica was one of the few places they didn't have a revolution every afternoon. Yeah, that was their best bet.

He knocked softly on Mac's door. There was no answer. But he heard sobbing sounds. So he tried the latch. It was open.

By the moonlight through her porthole, he could see Mac was face down on the bunk, crying. She still had her shirt on, but she'd kicked off her pants. Her small

177

boyish derriere was only partly covered by her shirt tail and her legs were fantastic.

She turned her head and peeked up at him from her pillow. She said, "Och, it's ye. Go away, Dick. Go find some bonny lassy to play with."

He moved over and sat down on the edge of the bunk as, despite her words, she unconsciously made room for him. He put a gentle hand on her sobbing shoulder and asked, "Hey, what's the matter, Mac?"

"Och, it's nothing for ye to frush over. I'm used to being lone and unwanted."

He said, "That's pretty dumb, coming from a beautiful girl, Mac."

"Ay, I noticed how bonny ye thought I was, when ye had yer way with them others."

"Hell, you made the offer, Mac. I was just extending common courtesy to those cute little pearl divers. I thought that was what you wanted me to do."

"Och, I thought I'd cry me eyes out from the shame I felt and the fool I'd acted."

"You didn't do anything to be ashamed of, kitten."

She sobbed louder and said, "I never get the chance! I'm almost twenty-five and nae man has ever wanted me! Can I tell ye a terrible secret, Dick?"

"Sure, that's what friends are for."

"Ye promise ye won't laugh?"

"Cross my heart. What is it?"

"Och, Dick, it's terrible. I'm still a virgin. I'll doubtless die a poor dried-up auld maid!"

He'd promised not to laugh, so he didn't, but it wasn't easy. He started running his hand down her spine as he said, "Hell, that's no real problem. But it sure is sort of surprising. You told me you'd fooled around and . . ."

"Och, I told ye it was a damned auld *girl* who offered to teach me about the facts of life. Did ye take me for a wee *queer,* for God's sake?"

He couldn't answer that without laughing like an idiot, either. So he just kept his mouth shut. He knew what a tomboy went through in any small town. She didn't want to hear he'd taken her for a man. A lot of crueler people had doubtless twitted Mac about her mannish look. It was funny, but as a man she looked effeminate, while as a woman she was pretty masculine. She was taller than the average girl and that short red hair didn't do a thing to soften her firm jaw and solid bone structure. He asked, gently, "Wasn't there ever a boy in Uruba who wanted to teach you the facts of life, Mac?"

"Och, those that cared for me at all only wanted to take me fishing. I fell in love too early with a bonny lad named Donald. I thought we were friends, but he married one of the damned auld Cameron sisters and never took me out to the pearling grounds again."

He said, "Donald sounds like an idiot." Then he rolled her over, bent down, and kissed her. Mac responded warmly, but as his hands started roaming she stiffened and said, "Fush! What are ye doing? Me blouse is open and it's half naked I am!"

He massaged her little breast, kneading the turgid nipple gently with his fingertips as he said, "I think you're beautiful, Flora."

"Och, call me Mac. I'm used to it, and I know ye're just trying to make me feel good."

"Yeah, you feel good as hell. You don't want me to stop, baby. And you don't want me to call you Mac and treat you like one of the boys, either. Relax, honey. I'm not going to hurt you."

"Ay, I ken what ye have in mind, Dick Walker. I'm not totally ignorant, even if I hadn't heard ye ravaging them other two right across yon companionway."

He kissed her again but moved his hand to neutral country just below her floating ribs. She was breathing hard, but she tried to keep it light as she asked, "Well, do ye deny it or noo?"

"Deny what, honey?"

"Dinna call me 'honey' unless ye mean it. I understand Carib and ye was doing terrible things to them lassies."

"Hell, they couldn't have minded much. Didn't they swim out to help me this afternoon?"

She laughed and said, "Ay, I noticed. I fear I only understood a wee bit of what was going on over there. Did ye really, well, make *both* of them feel bonny?"

179

He moved his cupped palm over her sharp hip bone and said, "It was just good clean fun. I'd show you, but . . . I don't know. Maybe we'd better not."

"Oh? Are ye saying ye'd rather have either of them than a great bony cow like meself?"

He said, "I'd love to get on your bones, baby. But this is sort of new to me, too. I'm not sure I want the responsibility of breaking in a frightened virgin."

"Och, who said I was frightened?"

"Aren't you?"

"Ay, terribly. If I had any sense I'd make ye leave. Ye have me fair mixed up. I've never been this close to a man before, with or without me pants on."

He lingered his hand on her flat white belly, thumb resting in her navel and fingertips just touching her pubic hairs. He knew in the light they'd be flaming red, and he knew if he didn't stop he wouldn't be able to. He said, "This is getting hard on both of us, Flora. I'm as confused as you are. I usually know where to go from here, but like I said, virgins make me nervous."

"I doubt ye could be feeling as nervous as me, right noo. Have ye had others like me, Dick?"

"Well, some."

"Ay, I figured as much, ye great bawdy thing. Did ye hurt them? I've ever heard it hurts, but other lassies seem to want it overmuch for a thing they find so painful."

He moved his hand smoothly down between her thighs, knowing she'd freeze if he tried to be sneaky. She gasped as his fingers caressed her moist turgid clit and he kissed her again to keep her from saying something dumb. She kissed back, but grabbed his wrist as if to move his hand away. Then, as she relaxed with a little sigh, her thighs parted in welcome and she began to help him with her own hand. He tongued her and didn't try to mount her. He knew she'd recover her senses, or her senseless fears, if he rushed things. She was begging for it with her body and thrusting instinctively. But he knew there was plenty of time and all of her was still waiting. So he just kissed and caressed her until she suddenly moaned and turned her face away to sob, "Och, what are

180

ye doing to me? I feel so queer and everything's spinning aroond!"

"Don't you like it?"

"I dinna ken. I do and I don't. Och, Dick, please don't. I mean, please don't stop. I mean, och ye're driving me mad and oooooooh!"

He kissed her ear and kept petting her, two fingertips inside, as she throbbed and sobbed her way back to reality. She suddenly rolled her head to kiss him, hungrily, and when they came up for air her eyes were shining up at his in the moonlight. She said, "That was wonderful. Was that what they call coming?"

"I hope so. I didn't get to feel it. How did you like the first lesson?"

"I said it was wonderful, but ye frightened me half to death. I'm afraid to ask for the next lesson. This takes a wee bit of getting used to."

He left his hand in place, but stopped moving it as he said, "I know. We can call it a night, if you don't want to go any further."

She blinked in surprise and asked, "We can? Me mother warned me that ye men are raging beasts, once ye've started. She told me that if I let a lad kiss me, alone, there was no telling where it would lead."

"That explains a lot, kitten. I don't want to hurt you and I don't want to frighten you. You may have had enough, for now."

She started moving his hand with her own as she sighed and said, "Och, I dinna think it would *kill* me to feel that again, if ye dinna mind."

He smiled down at her and said, "I do mind. I've got feelings, too. This is your last chance to stop the merry-go-round, kid."

"Ye mean ye still would, if I asked ye to?"

"Of course. But I can't promise to keep this up much longer."

She moved her hips teasingly and asked, "What would ye do if I told ye to leave?"

"I'd leave. Haven't you been paying any attention to me, Flora?"

"Awheel, it's fair hard to pay attention to *words*.

181

I dinna want ye to leave, Dick. I dinna want ye to stop, either, as well ye ken. Couldn't ye just pleasure me like this some more and satisfy yer cravings with Xixi or Xoxocatl as before?"

"Okay, but it's going to take both of them. I'm hotter than a two-dollar pistol tonight, and it's sure got to go somewhere!"

She sighed as she opened herself to his exploration and when he had three fingers in she giggled and said, "Och, that feels divine. I'll bet yer creature wouldn't feel any bigger, ye naughty thing."

He said, "Aw, shit, that does it," and sat up to fumble off his clothes with his free hand. She said, "Just a wee minute. What are you *doing?*"

He didn't answer as he peeled off his pants and moved to mount her. She protested, "I dinna think I'm ready for that!"

And then as he removed his hand and slid the real thing into her she gasped, "Och, I fear I'm being raped!"

He settled well in the saddle, moved experimentally, and said, "Yeah, how do you like it, so far?"

"Och, I want it as far as it'll go, ye bawdy brute. I love it and ye ken it. But I thought it was supposed to hurt."

He reached down and pulled a slim white thigh up to nestle against his ribs as Mac, or Flora, understood and did the same with her other leg on her own. He asked, "Does that hurt?" and she sobbed, "Nae, it feels marvelous and it's happening again and I'll die if ye stop."

So he didn't stop. He couldn't stop. Whoever it was who'd said meat was more tender close to the bone had been right on the money. The skinny little redhead was the best he'd had in months. She knew no acrobatic tricks and it was too early to suggest any. But once she'd started, she just gave herself, old-fashioned and innocently. He decided she wasn't the best he'd had in months after all. She was better. Any improvement would have killed him.

24

Gaston ran them up the river again and dropped anchor while Flora and Captain Gringo were having another orgasm. Gaston was too polite to knock on their door, of course. But they soon knew someone else had to be on watch.

Flora giggled in her lover's arms and whispered, "What is he *doing* to those twa lassies over there? They sound like they're killing one another!"

He patted her shoulder and took another drag on his cigar as he said, "Gaston is probably trying to teach them new tricks."

He had no idea what sort of tricks anyone could teach XiXi or Xoxocatl, but he was glad they had a new playmate. They'd taken his change in bed partners almost insultingly well. He'd been a little worried about that, having met some squaws a little more possessive.

After a while, they apparently exhausted the possibilities, even with Gaston, and it was possible to get a little sleep.

In the morning, after breakfast, XiXi and a less over-worked girl diver retrieved the Maxim gun from the river bottom. It was covered with slimy mud, of course. So he took it up to the foredeck and field stripped it.

The interior mechanism wasn't too bad. The parts just needed to be wiped off and oiled. The ammo belt was sort of soggy, but the ammo was supposed to be waterproof, so what the hell.

He spread the belt on the deck in the shade to dry. It was too bad about the boxes that had gone with *La Tortuga,* but he had almost two hundred rounds if push came to shove and there was plenty of ammo for the Gatling on the stern.

Flora joined him as he was putting the Maxim together. He noticed she was wearing a cotton skirt and off-the-shoulder blouse. She'd combed her hair in bangs, too. It did a lot for her. Apparently he'd convinced her she was pretty. No matter how things turned out, the boys in Port Uruba were in for a pleasant surprise.

She asked what he was doing and he said, "You can see I'm assembling a machine gun, honey. When you want to be with a guy, just admit it. It can save you a lot of fishing trips you didn't really want to go along on."

She laughed and said, "Och, if I ken ye, it's nae *fish* ye have in mind with any lass."

He shrugged and said, "I like girls. I'm not ashamed to say so."

"Ye mean what's passed between us is nae to be taken too seriously?"

"Honey, I take you serious as hell, in bed or not. I explained last night that I'm a knockaround guy on the run. So if you're after any promises, I'm afraid there's no way."

"Ay, I understand. I doubt my Athair would, though. I've been thinking about taking the three of ye to Uruba. I fear I *canna!* But I'm in noo hurry to leave, if ye're not. We've plenty of supplies and there's pearls here for the taking."

"Let's not worry about it, then."

"Dick, I'll share the pearls with ye. I'll take ye anywhere ye want to gae. I'll even stay with ye, if ye'll let me. But I canna give away the secrets of me clan."

He smiled and said, "Hey, don't cloud up and rain all over me. I said I understood, honey. We'll just stay here for now and enjoy the honeymoon while it lasts."

"Can't it last forever, Dick?"

"Nothing lasts forever and always is a lie. They call it a honeymoon because it usually takes a month before she starts wondering why he can't get a better job and he finds her snoring is getting on his nerves."

He saw he'd hurt her and said, "Sorry. I keep forgetting this is your first honeymoon. I like the way you've fixed your hair."

She hunkered down, glanced around to make sure they were unobserved, and took his hand in hers to place it between her thighs as she kissed him and said, "I'm going to devour ye tonight, ye brute."

"Have you forgotten *La Siesta?* Hold it, something's moving over on the shore."

He snapped the breechblock back in place and left the Maxim on the deck as he called out, "Gaston?"

"I see them," Gaston called from the cockpit.

Captain Gringo watched as a long ragged line of cotton-clad men materialized along the shoreline. They'd been spotted, too. He didn't turn his head to Flora as he said, "Move slow to the far side of the cabin. Make sure your girls stay under cover."

"Och, Dick, I want to help ye. But what are we facing? Who are yon men?"

"Beats me. If you want to help, do as I say, damn it. They look like bandits. I don't know what use they have for a schooner, but if they see a mess of naked women out here they'll be even more inspired."

Flora moved away as one of the men on shore waved his straw sombrero. Captain Gringo waved back casually and moved over to pick up the machine gun belt. He squatted over the Maxim, invisible from the shore, and fed the belt in as if he were fiddling with some fishing gear.

Bill Porter moved up the far side of the cabin and joined him. Porter glanced shoreward and said, "Gaston says he's leaving the tarp on the Gatling for now. But he's ready whenever you are. Can't we just zip out to sea?"

"If they're not looking for a fight we don't have to. If they are, they'll open fire the minute we start to weigh anchor."

"Can't we just cut the line?"

"With what? We don't have a cutting torch. Your so-called line is a steel chain. That's not our real problem, Bill. *Count* those sons of bitches!"

Porter said, "I can't. They keep coming out of the damned trees. Jesus, that's no bandit gang. It's a god-damned army!"

"I noticed. We may have to make a run for it. We'll soon find out. But we're broadside to them and they'll pepper us all the way down the channel, which is only the beginning of our troubles."

"Christ, there's more?"

"Yeah, glance casually seaward. In our infinite wisdom we moved up here around a couple of oxbow bends."

Porter did so and said, soberly. "Some guys have moved out on that point between here and the sea."

"That's what I just said. What we have here is what they used to call a Mexican Standoff in Texas."

"What do we do about it, Dick?"

"Beats the shit out of me. That's why they call it a standoff."

"Do you suppose we could radio for help?"

"Bill, you can't be that dumb. Who did you have in mind?"

"You're right. I lost my head. I thought, if they were bandits, somebody might be looking for them. But I guess *we'd* be considered bandits too, huh?"

"If not pirates. Hang on to your hat. The show is about to begin."

Porter stood by and watched as an improvised log raft put out from shore with a dozen men aboard. They were flying a white flag, or at any rate they'd nailed some guy's shirt to a pole. A couple of them wore mustard-colored uniforms. Most were in peon dress, spiffed up with crossed bandoleers of ammo and red sashes.

The raft paddled out to within hailing distance and an imposing figure in uniform called out, *"Buenos dias,* Señores. I am called General Puma and this is the Pana-manian Army Of Liberation."

Captain Gringo called back, "We're the schooner, *Cimarron,* out of Galveston. We're on a survey mission for an American engineering company. Dredging Incorpor-ated. You've probably heard of us?"

General Puma consulted with his followers as Porter murmured, "What was that all about? Who's looking for the *Thistlegorm?*"

"Nobody, *now*. You don't tell armed men you're a pearler. They might ask to see your pearls. We don't know for sure that none of the guys aboard *La Tortuga* survived, either. There's no lettering on our transom, thanks to Mac being sort of coy about her home port. A survey crew isn't likely to have much worth stealing and if he ever wins, he may want American friends, right?"

"Jesus, you think fast on your feet, Dick."

"You have to, in my business. Let's hope they buy it."

General Puma called out, "I wish for to come aboard, Señores."

"I'm sorry. Company policy. I can see who you are, and of course I trust you, but I have my orders."

"Orders? What is this nonsense about orders? *I* give the orders, here. Me, General Puma! We are coming aboard, like it or not!"

Captain Gringo bent, picked up the Maxim, and braced it on his hip to cover them as he replied, "I don't like it."

There was a moment of stunned silence. Then the leader aboard the raft said, "Well, since you put it that way, I will not inspect you after all."

They started to paddle backwards. But then General Puma raised his hand to stop them and called out, "Hey, I know who you must be. Only one man in Panama has ever been crazy enough to fire a machine gun from the hip. You are called Captain Gringo!"

"Maybe. What's it to you?"

"If you are Captain Gringo, my *mujer* is aboard that vessel. They told me my Catalina and the others left with Captain Gringo aboard a gunboat!"

"You've been out in the sun too long. Does this look like a gunboat?"

"Where is my Catalina? I warn you, if you have touched my woman, you will die!"

Captain Gringo didn't feel it would be polite to talk about a lady behind her back, dead or alive. So he shook his head and said, "You're barking up the wrong tree. I don't have any idea where your woman or any gunboat might be."

And then, as if to make a liar out of him, a gunboat came around the bend of the river from the sea, smoke funnel belching and moving fast!

Porter gasped, "Oh, shit, they *didn't* sink *La Tortuga!*"

Captain Gringo thought he was right, for a second. Then he saw the onrushing gunboat wasn't *La Tortuga*. For one thing, she was painted gray all over, and for another she was flying the Colombian flag and firing at the shoreline.

A shot from closer by rang out and a bullet whizzed by Captain Gringo's head as he realized the desperate men on the raft meant to board him as their only chance.

As chances went, it was lousy. He opened up with the machine gun on his hip and men, blood, and brains flew in every direction as he swept the raft clean. To his flank, Gaston was cranking the Gatling, aiming at the men on shore. Which was only fair, considering that any of them not shooting vainly at the armored gunboat were bouncing slugs off poor little *Thistlegorm*.

They both ceased firing as the gunboat slid between them and the shore to reverse her screws. Some white-clad officers in her conning tower were looking their way, sort of puzzled, but the gunboat was concentrating her fire on the shore, lobbing shells into the trees as the rebels moved back into the trees.

Flora came around the corner of the cabin, rifle in hand, and he saw she'd changed back to her sailor suit. She asked, "Who do ye want me to shoot?" and he snapped, "Nobody. Do you have a Colombian flag?"

"Ay, of course."

"Run it to the masthead, fast. Then get out your ship's papers, give them to me, and shut up! They're busy right now with the rebels they were sent to intercept. But they'll be boarding us any minute. I'd better do the talking."

25

Porter was doubled up inside with laughter, but Gaston only chuckled as they waved farewell to the government longboat when it rowed back to the Colombian gunboat. At Captain Gringo's side, Flora MacTavish said, "Thank the laird that's over. But ye had me in stitches, ye great mad fool! What did ye mean by mocking me Scottish brogue while them officers was aboard?"

"I wasn't mocking you. I was mocking them. I figured as long as I had to convince them I was one F.S. MacTavish I'd better sound like a bagpipe, and, what the hell, it worked."

"Och, ye didna sound like any Scot. Ye sounded like a music hall comic. I could hardly understand a word ye said."

Gaston nodded and said, "That, my child, is one of the reasons it worked. That poor English-speaking officer was too confused to ask as many questions as he might have. He was content to accept our heartfelt thanks for rescuing us from bandits and, as you see, they are leaving. I was afraid you'd say you knew they were General Puma's guerrillas, Dick. But I see you knew better."

Captain Gringo nodded and said, "Sure, if they don't have to share any rewards with us, they'll probably neglect to put our help in the official report. We'll let them move out and then we'd better weigh anchor ourselves. This cove is going to stink like hell in a while.

So a few hours later *Thistlegorm* stood out to sea with a cool breeze filling her sails and one of the Carib girls at the wheel. They weren't quite sure where they were bound, but it was a nice day and nobody was looking for them.

In Flora's cabin, Captain Gringo was giving his little friend another lesson and she was catching on fast. He'd been right about her being red-haired all over and she said she found the daylight spicy, too.

Across the companionway, XiXi, or maybe Xoxocatl, let out a loud shout of pure animal pleasure as Gaston did something that sounded obscene. The redhead in Captain Gringo's arms giggled and asked, "What do ye think he's doing to her now?"

"I don't know. She obviously likes it."

"Do ye think he makes love dirty, Dick?"

"Nothing's dirty between a man and a woman, unless it hurts."

"Oh. In that case, let's do something sort of dirty. I fear I have so much to learn, but I must say I find ye a braw teacher."

He laughed and said, "Well, we'll start with basic perversions and work our way up to Gaston's level, if we can last that long."

Meanwhile, out in the lounge, Bill Porter was trying to ignore the slap and tickle games all around. The burley exbanker had too much on his mind to think of sex, even if he hadn't been so in love with his young wife. He knew his Athol was probably dying. He was afraid she despised him for running off like that instead of staying to face the music like a man. He knew he'd learned to despise himself. But the last few days had made him face up to life in the raw, and somehow it didn't seem so awful to stand trial on a minor felony. Bill Porter had decided to go back. Athol needed him. He'd face them down and take his lumps. If he went to jail he went to jail. He just wanted to get it over with.

But he knew his desperately ill wife would need money while he was away. Athol had often asked him why he didn't try to put some more of his jokes and crazy stories he liked to tell on paper.

Porter went to Flora's writing desk and sat down. He found paper and pencil, but hesitated. He knew he'd never be a great author, but maybe some of his amusing observations would be worth printing.

He thought of the past few crazy days, and of the other soldiers of fortune he'd met down here. He couldn't just write it as it had happened. Nobody would ever believe it. But if he took a bit here and a bit there and wrote with tongue in cheek . . . But could he sign his real name? Who was going to buy a story from a convicted felon? He'd use a pen name.

And so, as as *Thistlegorm* sailed on, he picked up the pencil and carefully blocked out

CABBAGES AND KINGS
BY O. HENRY

"THE KING OF THE WESTERN NOVEL" is MAX BRAND